CHRISTMAS COMES BUTCH ONCE A YEAR

EVERNIGHT PUBLISHING ®

www.evernightpublishing.com

SAM CRESCENT

Copyright© 2023 Sam Crescent

ISBN: 978-0-3695-0812-6

Cover Artist: Sour Cherry Designs

Jacket Design: Jay Aheer

Editor: Karyn White

CHRISTMAS COMES BUTCH ONCE A YEAR

DEDICATION

To all of my readers for their patience. I hope you love this one.

CHRISTMAS COMES BUTCH ONCE A YEAR

CHRISTMAS COMES

ONCE A YEAR

The Skulls, 16

Sam Crescent

Copyright © 2018

Chapter One

Knocking back his second glass of whiskey for the evening, Butch knew he should be at home with his wife, Cheryl. She needed him now more than ever. They were getting close to that date when she'd give birth to their first child. They'd had several miscarriages between them, and even though he considered Michael his son, he, in fact, belonged to another man, another club brother who Butch was trying to get along with.

Not that it was hard.

He wasn't in Fort Wills anymore and hadn't been for years.

He still wore the Fort Wills patch and was still a member, but he hadn't been back home in so long now, at least not to stay. Nope, that was for people that didn't break their loyalty. Not that he ever *wanted* to be disloyal to The Skulls, but he had been. He had his reasons, and those who knew him and his situation were well aware of them.

The biggest surprise for him was Lacey.

They kept in touch.

They were the only two surviving members of a previous MC, one that had been slaughtered, and the name of which he refused to voice again. It was hard at times not to think about what had happened over the years. For the longest time The Skulls had been his life. Part of his very fucking soul, and now, there were days, he felt like he was no more than Ned Walker's personal protector.

There was no other word for it. It sucked, big time.

Running a hand down his face to clear the feeling he was experiencing, he tapped the rim of his glass for the bartender to know he needed a refill.

"You know, being here alone, drinking, is not good for a man's soul," Ned said, taking a seat beside him at the bar.

"Do you have some kind of radar for where I'm at?" Butch didn't even bother to turn to look at the much older man. He must be nearing his eighties, but no one actually knew how old Ned was.

Whenever he tried to find out information about the old man, nothing ever came up. Ned had his hand in so many pies it was fucking scary. From drugs, to fighting, to guns, and other shit that he didn't want to think about, Ned was the go-to for most deals in Vegas.

"Don't you have people to kill?"

"Probably, but you see, I've got you to think about."

"You're not going to pretend to me that you care,

old man."

Ned put a hand over his heart. "Damn, son, that hurt."

Rolling his eyes, Butch watched the bartender fill up his shot glass.

"That's his last for the night," Ned said.

"Yes, sir."

"I'm right fucking here, and I didn't say it was my last one."

"You've got a wife at home that is freaking out twenty-four seven, and I'm not having you hungover on the jobs that I need you to do. Last drink, or do you want to take this outside?"

Butch stared at his glass and figured he could take the old man. However, there were so many rumors when it came to Ned. Some people thought he had some kind of mystic voodoo on his side or at least *something* that always made sure he won.

The thing about Ned, no one had ever bested him unless they played dirty. The only time he could recall was when Tabitha, Ned's granddaughter, was a young one, and they'd been attacked. They'd hurt Tabitha, even as they took down Ned.

Thinking about everything he'd experienced with his time of being in The Skulls, it was a wonder he was still sane.

"You've got to get home."

"I'm going to. Can't a man have a drink after a long day at work?" Instead of knocking the entire thing back, he sipped at it, refusing to rush the pleasure of enjoying his drink.

"You know, when Tiny made the decision for you to come here, I thought it was a big mistake."

"I fucked up," Butch said. "It was necessary."

"You've proven to them your loyalty. Enough

time has passed, and you've done what is right now. You can't keep bringing up the past. They know everything, and you're not keeping any secrets anymore. We're living life the way we have to. It's the way the world works. No one can hold that against you."

"You keep secrets from Eva?"

Eva was his daughter and married to Tiny.

"Fuck yeah. Of course, I did. I still do. There's a lot of shit in this life that she doesn't need to know."

Butch wasn't about to tell him that Eva was sharp as anything and had probably already figured out everything he'd kept from her. That was for him to discover.

Checking the time, he saw it was a little after eleven. He hoped Cheryl was fast asleep.

They were into their eighth month, and because of all the other failed pregnancies, they'd agreed not to have sex.

Only, that came at a cost.

He'd never cheat on his woman. Not once.

Pregnancy did something to a woman. Even if a woman was calm before her pregnancy, that wasn't going to stay with their personality.

Cheryl was … paranoid as fuck.

Not only that, she was afraid he was cheating on her, which made it difficult going home. All he wanted to do was to wrap his arms around her, protect her, tell her it was going to be okay.

He didn't know if that was even true, but he liked to think he could do that for the woman he loved.

Arguing with her caused her stress. The last thing he wanted to do was get into an argument about nothing, because he'd never cheat, and then for her to lose the baby over nothing.

"I remember when Eva's mother was pregnant

with her. That bitch was so fucking high most of the time, but when she had Eva, I kept her off the dope. Up until that point, she was a decent lay. Imagine having no drugs, heavily pregnant, and just fucking miserable. That was Eva's mom. The biggest lie I ever told Eva?" Ned stopped, looking at his hands that were flat on the counter.

"What was it?" Butch asked.

Like so many people before him, he'd been lulled in by Ned's conversation. By his memories.

Women loved the old bastard. Cheryl loved having him around for dinner, especially now that Michael had moved back to Fort Wills with his father.

They'd been able to have a lot of time on their own since he'd been gone. It was a hard decision to make.

Michael was an angry child, and seeing as Alex complained all the time about having no time with him, it seemed like a good idea. Of course, he'd not thought about how it would affect Cheryl.

She missed her son, and Butch did as well, even if he was an evil bastard at times that liked to cause nothing but trouble.

"I told Eva that her mom wanted her. That she would be so damn proud of her, and the truth is, Eva's mom wanted to fucking kill her. I had to have her watched twenty-four-seven so she didn't try and kill herself or our baby." Ned sighed. "That's what you get when you fuck up."

Butch had no idea. "Did you always love Eva?"

"The moment I saw her, I loved her. She's my flesh and blood. Of course, she has the worst taste in men, but then, it wasn't like I'd picked out anyone better for her. At least she's been able to train Tiny. He's doing well. A good son-in-law even if he does make bad decisions."

"Lash is a damn good Prez, and you know it."

"That I do know; however, when I want a job done right, I want to rely on people I can trust. The Skulls and Chaos Bleeds were two MC clubs I can trust. Now, I'm test driving everyone."

The Skulls and Chaos Bleeds had both come away from the drug and gun runs. After years of facing one enemy or making new ones, they'd decided to go legit. They had some deals going with the Billionaire Bikers MC as well as witness protection programs. They helped men, women, and children all over the country.

It's what the club did.

Butch wished he'd been part of it, but again, he was back in Vegas, knowing his true purpose was here. Even when he missed the club life, the brotherhood, that sense of purpose, Fort Wills would never be his home again.

"Go on home, Butch. Snuggle up with your wife, and if she gives you shit about cheating, kiss the fuck out of her, so she knows there's no pussy you want to be in but hers."

Knocking back his drink, he shook his head. "I don't have a clue how you manage to get women to fall all over you."

Ned stuck his tongue out and gave it a wiggle. "I'm a fucking hero."

"You're disgusting."

"To get a woman eating out of your hand, you must first be willing to eat them." Ned winked at him, and Butch turned his back.

It would have been nice to eat his wife's pussy. They were both so filled with worry that there was no chance it was going to happen.

****

Cheryl ran the brush through her hair for the hundredth time and stared at her reflection. She was way too pale, and there was no way she'd be putting makeup on in the hope of looking healthy.

Placing a protective hand over her stomach, she tried not to cry.

When she got pregnant with Michael, it had been a mistake, an accident. After one night with a stranger only to be left to raise her child alone, she never for a second thought she would have trouble delivering again.

Only, she had.

She and Butch had tried and failed so many times.

Putting the brush down, she stared at her reflection, feeling sick to her stomach. They'd never gotten this far before, and seeing as they'd had a couple of miscarriages along the way, their doctor was on constant call just in case something went wrong.

She stood up and stared at her enormous stomach.

It stuck right out in front of her, looking odd.

She put her hand underneath her breasts and curved over the bump. It still amazed her even now that she was heavily pregnant.

So far, no scares.

The loneliness of this pregnancy though, killed her.

Butch didn't spend a whole lot of time with her, and when he came home, he always looked tired.

He worked hard for Ned Walker and all those fighters, but she hated it. She'd been to the gym where they all trained and had seen all the young, beautiful, sexy women who were hanging around. She'd even walked in on several of the women giving head to the men, or taking it in the pussy or ass.

Right now, she'd give anything to just feel her

man's arms wrapped around her, his lips on her neck.

Instead, she wondered if he'd been lured in by one of the pieces of ass that was always around.

"You know you're thinking stupid thoughts." Sitting on the edge of the bed, she saw it was late and only getting later.

Butch had started to come home later and later. Not that she blamed him. Even as she threw accusations at him, it drove her crazy, and she was always overcome by guilt once it was all over. She felt like a horrible person for some of the stuff she'd said to him.

Covering her face with her hands, she wondered if it was even any use in trying to figure out how to fix them.

She was going to be giving birth within the next month, and there were times the similarities between this pregnancy and Michael's weren't lost on her.

Only she didn't love Alex.

Her heart belonged to Butch.

She would die for him without batting an eye.

He owned her very soul.

Now, though, everything was going so weirdly. She didn't know how to stop this divide that was happening between them.

It was all because of this baby right now.

They'd experienced so much heartache in having a baby that it terrified her to fail once again. Butch was not only an amazing man but a truly wonderful father. He'd been there for Michael every single step of the way, even when he got in trouble.

She pushed some of her hair that had fallen onto her face out of the way. Getting to her feet, she made her way slowly downstairs to the kitchen. There was nothing in this world that a little hot chocolate wouldn't fix. This wouldn't be as good as Angel could do it, but she knew how to fix a hot chocolate to take away all of her woes.

Moving out to Vegas should have been a fresh start for all of them.

At first, she really thought they could make it work, and they had. Ned Walker had been with them every single step of the way, and there were times he was more of a father to them than anything else.

Of course, his group of fighters were part of their world as well. They'd lost many men along the way, and there were times she didn't think she could handle being part of this world.

Just as she was pouring the steaming hot chocolate into her cup, she heard the door open and close.

Her heart sped up, and as Butch came around the corner into the kitchen, he stopped. He looked tired all the time. She didn't know what to say, which was another problem they were facing.

He threw his keys onto the table, and she watched as he ran a hand down his face. "You should be in bed."

Gritting her teeth, she didn't want to snap at him or do anything to start an argument. Instead, she smiled and offered up her cup. "I just wanted to get a drink." She tilted her head to the side, watching him. "There's nothing wrong with having some hot chocolate. I made enough for two cups." He didn't tell her to stop, so she got him a cup and poured the rest inside. Next, she added a good handful of marshmallows. She hated the sweet stuff, but she knew Butch loved it.

They both sat down at the table, and she was sure to lower herself into the chair. It had been a couple of weeks since she'd looked even a little dignified while she tried to sit or stand.

"Did you have a good day?" she asked.

"It was long. Fucking tiring. Another fighter

smashed through Carlton. He's in the hospital at the moment."

"Was this an actual fight?"

"Nah, not even close. It was one of Ned's fighters that put Carlton down. He was shouting shit about how good he was, how much better than everyone else. People don't want or need to hear that, so he got slugged. It disappointed Ned. Carlton was supposed to be able to take a few hits. One punch and he's down isn't going to cut it in the ring."

Some women would be really upset by the kind of work Butch did. He helped men to train in illegal fighting. The thing was, she knew all about his past, the truth of The Skulls, and deep down, she'd love him no matter what he did.

The fights were going to happen regardless. She only hoped Butch never got involved. Taking care of this baby alone didn't exactly appeal to her.

Butch released a sigh, and she smelled the whiskey on his breath.

"I went out for a drink after I dumped Carlton's useless ass in the hospital."

"It's fine." She'd noticed he preferred to go out to the bar rather than come home to her. "I'm sorry."

"What are you sorry for?"

"For everything. For this baby, for … being a total bitch to you." The hormones were kicking in once again, and as she sniffled, she heard Butch groan.

"Don't, babe. You know I can handle everything in the world but not that. Please." He got out of the chair and moved behind her. He wrapped his arms around her as best he could. His lips were against her neck.

She missed him so much, missed his touch. "I don't mean to push you away."

"You're not. I'm going to the bar to give you a

chance to rest. There's no other woman. I've told you that a gazillion times, and I'll keep on telling you that. There's no one else in this world I'll want but you."

"But I'm an elephant. Look at me." She placed a hand over her stomach. "I can't satisfy you. I can't do anything but look like this, and I'm so afraid of losing this baby. I don't want you to hate me."

Before she could say anything more, Butch had dragged the chair so that he could face her. He knelt down before her and forced her to look at him.

"Now, you listen to me, baby. I don't hate you. I can never hate you. I want this baby, too, and I know how important it is to the both of us. I get that you're full of your pregnant mom hormones. I'm not going to cheat. I'm not going to walk away. You're not getting rid of me that easily. Once we have our kid in our arms, Ned doesn't know this yet, but he's taking care of our child while I spend the weekend fucking you and making you aware who you belong to. Of course, when the doctor says we can. Do you understand me?"

"I just … we're here because of me, and everything is a mess."

"No, we're here because of *me*."

"Do you want to go back?" she asked.

She saw him hesitate, and then he kissed her.

Even though that's all they'd been doing for eight months, it still had her heart racing.

"What I want right now is to put you in bed, wrap my arms around you, and sleep."

Chapter Two

Circling the gym, Butch watched each hit, assessing where the fighters' weaknesses were, and what they were doing that would inevitably get them killed. There were some men who were just training as fighters, but some wanted the notoriety of being the best Ned Walker fighter there was.

He'd never fought in the ring, but he knew without a doubt there were only a couple of men who'd survive that ring and that was purely because they'd survive going through the rounds with him.

Butch wasn't even tempted to compete. His moments of fighting had come and gone.

Besides, he was a family man. He had to provide.

"He's a piece of shit. I'm going to fucking kill him if he comes around here again. I've had enough of his mouth." Javier came to stand beside him.

Cruz and Mistletoe were with him.

"Who are you talking about?" Butch asked.

These were three of the best fighters they had. They'd been in the ring a minimum of ten times each, and for a fighter without any rules, that was some serious strength right there.

"Carlton," Cruz said. "I can't believe how Javier just clocked him, man. I thought he'd get up, but yet, the sucker just went pop and he was out."

Butch had witnessed Carlton's fall and also Ned's pissed-off attitude. It wasn't good when a fighter was out of it in one punch.

"Best expression I seen on that fucker's face," Mistletoe said, and proceeded to show off a knocked-out look.

Shaking his head, he watched another fighter. He was young, eighteen, and as far as Butch was concerned, he shouldn't have even been competing. However, Ned had his own rules and as such, he was training.

There's no way he'd be ready in time for the Christmas round of fighting.

In the back of his mind it sickened him that they were even having a Christmas fight. The stakes were always even higher as most of the earnings went to the fighter as a bonus for drumming up all the excitement.

Of course, Ned took his cut at the door, but he raised the bar for entry so that there was plenty of dough for the fighter without his cut being lowered.

"How's the wife?" Javier asked.

"Fine."

"I've been meaning to stop by, say hi, but the last time she was there, she dropped a jug and burst into tears."

"She did? When?" Panic filled his chest as the last time she'd dropped anything or done something like that, she'd been in pain.

"Oh, this was a good few weeks ago. She knocked her hand on the fridge door as she pulled it out. It dropped out of her hand, smash. I cleaned up the mess real quick, but she was still crying. Sobbing, and I don't do women that cry. Sorry. I get the hell out of there, real quick." Javier shook his head as if it was the most logical thing in the world to dodge a woman crying.

Butch sighed. "It's the hormones."

"Yeah, she said that, and I don't trust that shit. Women with hormones or anything wrong with them, it's crazy shit. You need to learn, man, just get out of there."

Butch chuckled.

"How much longer you got?" Mistletoe asked.

"She's due to give birth the day of the fight."

"So, you're not going to be here to see who wins or loses?" Cruz asked.

He shook his head. "My wife needs me."

Before she got pregnant, Cheryl would come around the gym all the time. She'd pass out items she'd baked, and talk with everyone that was around. She was considered part of the fold, but when her pregnancy started to show, Ned put his foot down.

Fights erupted all the time, and they didn't want her to get hurt.

Butch didn't want her to get in the line of fire, which was why he hadn't fought Ned about it.

It meant he missed her throughout the day. He loved seeing her smiling face, and he imagined this distance between them was partly caused by that. He had a job to do.

If they were in Fort Wills, it wouldn't be a problem.

There weren't a lot of women for Cheryl to hang with here. She didn't make friends easily, and even in the neighborhood, she wasn't too social.

"This kid is not ready," Javier said, sighing. "It's a shame. He's got real … passion."

Butch saw too many easy moves that would put the kid on his ass.

Climbing into the ring, he heard a loud chorus of hollers and shouts as people started to gather around the ring. He didn't bother pulling on any gloves.

"What are you doing?" Punk asked.

That was the name he wanted to be called, Punk. His punk ass was going to get killed that was for sure.

"This is my stage, man. I don't need you on here, showing off."

Butch didn't say a word to Punk.

Butch nodded at the other fighter who was helping to train, and the kid left the ring, leaving him facing Punk.

He didn't even raise his fists as he stepped up to him.

Ned had come out of his office to see.

"What the fuck?" Punk asked. "You fucking mute? Why ain't you speaking to me?"

"It's a fight, asshole," Javier said. "You think every fighter is going to come up to you and give you a kiss?"

"I'd keep an eye on him if I was … you."

While Punk was distracted, Butch landed his first shot, straight in the face.

No gloves.

Pure flesh on flesh.

Punk went down, a hand to his face. "Fuck!"

"The one thing you should always, always fucking know is never, ever take your eyes off the target." Butch stepped back. "Get up. I didn't hit you that hard, otherwise you'd be out of it. Come on, I want you on your feet when you face me."

Punk got to his feet, but after another punch, he went down again.

Ned stepped a little closer to the ring.

"You think you're ready for the Christmas fight. Right now, I can hear booing coming from all around us. You can't even give them a good fight."

"You're not playing fair. You're not suited up."

"Reality check, kid. You won't be playing fair in the ring." To prove his point, he grabbed the back of Punk's head, lifting him to his feet. "None of the fights are fair in the ring. It's why they pay so fucking much. Men and women want to see a bloodbath. They want to see every single punch landing on bare flesh. The bruises starting to form, to enhance and highlight the sheer fucking savagery of what's happening right in front of them. Every punch you give, you're being assessed. This one fight will start your next one, if you live long enough to tell the fucking tale, and right now, you're not going to do that unless you start fucking trying."

He slammed Punk down and stepped back, waiting. "Come on, get up."

Punk got up, and for the next half an hour, Butch proved to the entire gym exactly why Punk shouldn't go for the Christmas beating. It just wasn't right. It was boring, and if the men were booing, it meant the fighter was nowhere near ready to promote to the fucking buyers, the people who paid them to be fucking mean.

Who wanted to see blood more than a living, breathing man.

With that, he got out of the ring and nodded at Javier. "Teach him a thing or two."

He moved toward Ned.

"I was right," Butch said.

"You were right."

"If you put that kid forward for a fight, he'll be dead within ten minutes. They're not trained to hold back. He's dead if you allow it to continue."

"I've already taken him out of the running. Problem is, he needs money." Ned looked toward him.

"He does?"

"Mom, cancer. She's in the hospital, and bills are mounting fast. Why do you think a good kid like him is even fighting like this?" Ned shook his head. "I wanted to help him."

"Why not give him the money?" Butch asked.

"Can't do that. Word gets out that I give charity, they'll be around here all the damn time and I don't give shit away for free." Ned turned away and headed into his office.

And that was one of the reasons Ned had lasted so fucking long. He didn't give anything to anyone for free. He had no fucking heart, and right now, Butch couldn't blame him.

Give something to one, and they'd all want a piece.

****

"I'm guessing you're not used to having guests?" Lacey asked.

Cheryl placed down the cup of coffee as well as a sandwich she'd just made for Lacey. It wasn't often she got a guest, and certainly not one that she liked.

Lacey was Whizz's old lady and had a life back in Fort Wills. She always made sure to visit though. Lacey and Butch were the last surviving members of the Savage Brothers MC, which was completely wiped out by their enemy and then by The Skulls.

"I don't do guests."

"Is this because of your pregnant self or because you just don't like people?"

"A mixture of both. I don't … the women on the street are always around here if Butch is here. They don't pay me attention unless he's here, and I'm not going to even try to make friends knowing they want my husband's dick."

"Look at you, saying such big words."

Cheryl's cheeks heated.

"It's fine, it's fine," Lacey said, laughing. "I did wonder why you never swore."

"I've spent a lot of time with Michael, and I didn't want him to pick up bad habits."

Lacey started laughing.

"What? What is it?"

"Just the thought of Michael being a good kid. He swears all the time."

"And Alex doesn't stop him?" Cheryl felt the anger filling up inside her. Alex was supposed to be able to handle their son. It was why she'd asked for him to take him. He wasn't happy with her, and she knew he missed his father. He was in that teenage stage where everyone and everything else was an asshole and the only person who was right about anything and everything was himself.

All kids went through it, but with pregnancy and how much time Butch was with Ned, she needed the help. Alex hadn't spent all that much time with Michael and she thought it would really work, but if he was acting out, then that couldn't be right.

"Alex keeps Michael in line and if not him, the other kids do."

"What do you mean?" Cheryl asked.

"They're Skull kids, Cheryl, honey. Michael's bad attitude wasn't taken very well. They put him in his place. It's what the kids do. Nothing and no one comes between them."

Cheryl took a deep breath.

"You really do need to relax. Your son is in good hands, and you know you can come to Fort Wills any time, right?"

She shook her head. "It's just ... I don't feel like that's my place anymore. Everything got so fucked up, and this is our home now, you know."

"I get it. It *is* your home. I love being in Fort Wills though. I know we're protected there," Lacey said.

Cheryl chuckled. "We're protected here. Butch seems to instill that loyalty thing where people are willing to step in front of him and take a bullet. It's quite scary when I think about it."

"I bet. Butch would have made a damn good Prez, that's for sure."

"Do you ever think about what could have been if the Savage Brothers were still living?" Cheryl asked.

There were a few times she saw Butch holding his leather cut, and she wondered if he missed the patch of his previous club.

"Sometimes I think what could have been. We all had something taken from us, and that wasn't fair, nor was it right." Lacey sighed, gripping her neck. "I don't know. The truth is, we didn't have it in us to become something. Butch did. He's always been a fighter, and I think I got lucky by falling in love with Whizz. If it'd not been with him, I'd be dead as everyone else. Do you think Butch misses being with The Skulls all the time?"

Cheryl blew out a breath. "I honestly don't have a clue. I mean, sometimes I think I see him yearning to be part of it all again, and other times, he doesn't seem to care. I know he's damn good with the fighters. I see the respect the guys have for him. He's got a little following there. Of course, there's also the women that hang out, but I try not to think about that."

Lacey burst out laughing. "What you need to do is when you drop this young one, go there and show them who has him by the balls. They'll all step back. Believe me. There's nothing better than letting a woman know where a man's dick belongs."

"You do that with Whizz?"

"Don't have to. Unless it's got a keyboard and code, I know I'm safe."

Cheryl threw her head back, laughing. She couldn't remember the last time she'd laughed so loud and so hard. Putting a hand on her swollen stomach, she thought how good it felt to smile.

"Can I touch?" Lacey asked.

She knew the other woman couldn't have children. She'd been gang-raped as a child, and it had ruined any chance of her ever having children, which was why she'd adopted three so far.

Her love of children, of family, was always clear to see.

"Of course."

Lacey moved to the chair closer to her and put her hand on her stomach. Seeing the wonder, joy, and envy on her face filled Cheryl with sadness.

She was pregnant and having a healthy child if what the doctors said was true. Lacey would never have that experience, never know what it was like to go full-term with a baby.

"I'm so sorry," Cheryl said.

Tears filled Lacey's eyes. "Don't be."

"If you cry and Whizz finds out, he'll kill me."

Lacey chuckled. "Nah, he'd put your pension somewhere else or change your child's name."

She couldn't help but laugh. Whizz was like his name suggested, a whiz on the computer. His mad skills had helped The Skulls and Ned a few times.

"It's good having you here." She placed her hand over Lacey's.

"Yeah, I don't come all that often, and I really should. I love being with you and of course, Butch."

Lacey had come on her own this time, and as her baby kicked, Cheryl moved Lacey's hand to that part of her stomach. "Oh, wow."

"Yeah, it can go from being 'oh, wow' to 'oh, fuck, that hurts.'"

"Do you know what you're having yet?"

She shook her head. "Nope. We were going to find out the sex so we could do the spare bedroom, but after we learned the sex of our last one and started to paint the room pink, and then I lost … her, we decided against it."

"You have suffered so much," Lacey said.

"I haven't. So many women go through this, and

then, like you, you can't have any. I'm blessed to have this, and I know that."

Pulling Lacey into a hug, she wouldn't let her go.

"You know I'm not a touchy-feely kind of person," Lacey said, but didn't make a move to pull out of the hug.

"I don't care."

The sound of the door opening and closing had her letting Lacey go to breathe. Seconds later, Butch appeared. He didn't look tired this time.

He smiled at her and then laughed.

"I should have known your crazy ass was here."

Lacey got to her feet and moved to Butch.

They didn't have an awkward reunion because Butch simply pulled her into his arms. "Damn, it has felt like a lifetime, honey. Look at you, all grown up." He held Lacey at arm's length.

Cheryl chuckled as Lacey rolled her eyes.

"I'm not a child, you know."

"Yeah, well, how you do your hair, it makes me wonder."

Cheryl ran her fingers through her own dull locks. She'd been wanting to get a haircut for some time.

"I saw that, honey. Don't you worry at all. I've got my styling stuff in my bag. I figured I'd stay for the weekend and get you looking like a living person rather than the dead."

"I don't look that bad," she said.

"True, but you could look better." Lacey turned to Butch and punched him in the arm.

"Ow, why did you do that?"

"Look at your wife? She's like a damn ghost, she's so pale. You should be ashamed of yourself. She needs to get out more, and being the caring husband that you are, you need to be the one to help her go for a walk, catch some sun, or do something. I hold you personally responsible for that."

Butch rubbed his arm. "Want me to make dinner?" he asked.

"Chicken is in the fridge."

"I'll do that while you two get pampered and be your lovely selves." He hugged Lacey again. "It's good to have you here." He tapped her back before moving toward Cheryl. When his lips brushed across hers, she felt that heat rising up inside her, building. She wanted him.

"Love you."

"Love you too."

She watched him leave the room and looked at Lacey.

"You totally want to hit that," Lacey said.

"You're a goofball. I have hit that." She pointed at her stomach.

Lacey started gyrating her hips, and she just burst out laughing.

Everything was good.

She and Butch would be more than fine so long as they just took some time for themselves.

Chapter Three

One week later

Butch repeatedly hit the punching bag. He had to get all this need out of his system. It was driving him crazy. Ever since Lacey had left town, there was something going on between him and Cheryl, and he had to put some focus on that shit.

The gym was completely empty apart from Ned working in his office. Sweat poured off him as he imagined his wife.

His beautiful, sexy, alluring wife with her long, brown hair, stunning eyes, and pregnant stomach.

He found it hard to imagine his life without her.

Eight months they'd been without sex.

Eight long and lonely months.

Holding her was both a blessing and a curse.

All he wanted to do was fuck her, to show her how much he craved and desired her. Only he held himself back, constantly waiting, letting her set the pace so he didn't hurt her.

He'd held her through two miscarriages, and then she'd admitted she'd been pregnant another time but she hadn't told him about it for fear of losing the baby.

Every second of this pregnancy he'd been fucking terrified.

They could only handle so much grief before it completely tore them apart.

"Last time I checked, you had a wife," Ned said.

Butch didn't stop punching the bag in front of him.

After a few seconds, Ned grabbed the bag, holding it firmly. Again, he didn't have a clue what the guy's age was, but he held that bag as if it didn't have any weight in it.

As Butch hit it several times, Ned tutted.

"So, this is what you do all day and you wonder why your marriage is in trouble."

"You've never been married, so you don't get to tell me how to deal with my problems."

Ned held his hands up. "Clearly, what you're doing right now is working."

"What do you want from me, old man? Seriously."

"I think the biggest question here, Butch, is what do *you* want?"

Silence fell between them.

Ned chuckled.

"You see, in this world there are two kinds of people. There are those people that do everything, and then there are those that sit around blaming everyone else for how shit their life is."

Butch rolled his eyes. "I don't have time for this."

"You have all the time in the world. You spend a lot of time here already, nothing wrong with taking a few more minutes to listen to some advice."

"Who the fuck do you think you are? My dad?"

"Nah, if I was your dad I'd have put you over my knee when you were a snot-nosed kid." Ned pointed a finger in his face. "You have everything at your fingertips. Your entire life ahead of you and you're wasting it for what? Why the fuck are you here?"

"Because I fucked up! Is that what you want me to say? To be honest with you. I fucked up, which is why I landed myself here with you." He glared at Ned. "I had to take my punishment, and not only that, I dragged Cheryl down with me."

"Down? Where the fuck are you down? I don't see anything down about your situation. You've got a wife that thinks the world of you. A baby on the way.

Life's been tough, but here's a newsflash, no one owes you shit. You want what you want, and you take it. Simple as that."

Butch shook his head and started to walk away.

"Here's a question for you, Butch, you think you could go back?"

This made him pause.

"What?"

"To Fort Wills. You think you could sit at the table in your fancy church meeting, listening to Lash?"

"What the hell does this have to do with anything?" Butch asked.

Ned stared at him. "You've been on your own for a long time now, Butch. Longer than a lot of men are away from their clubs unless they're part of the Nomad chapter. You're your own boss. You make the rules here. What makes you think you could go back to taking orders? You look around you and you see this as a punishment? This is fucking freedom right here. The only problem right now is you've not got the balls to take what you want."

With that, Butch walked right up to him and, old man or not, landed a blow to the bastard's face. Ned didn't go down.

"Stay the fuck away from me."

"You know I'm right. That's what has you worried. Why you keep looking at the door?"

"I check the door because of Cheryl."

"Bullshit. You check the door to see if you've finally got your orders to return. Here's a little thought, you ever think that you may not *want* to return?"

"What the hell are you talking about?"

"You're a bright man, Butch. Figure it out, but I have a feeling your bad mood has nothing to do with your wife, but about the harsh reality of the truth you're refusing to face." Ned rubbed his chin and Butch watched him walk away, staring at him.

He didn't linger in the gym. He wanted to get home. Storming out the door, he didn't go quietly. Climbing into his car, he sat, holding the wheel, squeezing it as if it had the answers to all of his problems.

Nothing was simple anymore.

His life had never been easy. He'd accepted that.

But what the hell was wrong with him?

He and Cheryl were doing good. Apart from the yearning on his part and the fact she was pregnant, they were in a really good place.

The only problem was, something bothered him.

He didn't like this sinking feeling that twisted inside his gut.

Glancing to the passenger side of his car, he stared at his leather cut.

His Skulls jacket. The one he still wore, even though he wasn't in Fort Wills.

Picking it up, he spread it out over the steering wheel and ran his hand across the emblem and logo.

Becoming part of The Skulls had felt like the right path to go on. He'd been part of an MC. His father had been Prez and he his brat a lifetime ago. When he'd gotten pushed into the care system and it had been stripped away from him, part of his soul had died. When he took on the role of Prospect at The Skulls, it had felt … exhilarating. He'd finally woken up to what he wanted, what he needed to be, and where he needed to go.

An MC wasn't just a damn biker club.

It was family, and that's what he missed about The Skulls.

Could he go back?

Was that even possible?

Being in Vegas, working with Ned, doing what he needed to do to make a living, it had changed him.

He didn't like where Ned's questions were going. It scared him.

His options were fading out, and part of him was afraid of what Cheryl wanted. He didn't want to bring it up in case they weren't on the same page.

Dropping the jacket back on the seat, he slammed his hand against the steering wheel. No matter how hard he tried, he seemed to be fucked whatever he did.

Collapsing back against his seat, he closed his eyes.

"Just take a deep breath. It'll all be fine. Perfectly fine."

Opening his eyes, he stared at Ned, who stood in front of the car. He didn't want to talk to the old bastard right now.

Ned came to the driver's side of the car. "You done having your temper tantrum?"

"Yeah, what is it?"

"I need a ride to the hospital. Punk got into a fight. He's hurt."

"What?" Butch sat up, but Ned had already closed the door and rounded to the passenger side.

He threw the leather cut into the back seat and sat down. Starting up the car, he pulled out, and headed toward the hospital. "That kid is too young to fight," Butch said.

"I know that. You know that. I'll see how badly he's been messed up and see what the damage is. So I can deal with the consequences."

"Always thinking about your reputation."

"If one person thinks they can take out my fighters, how long before my gym gets hit? My businesses? You think people show me respect because I'm old. Hell, no, they show me respect because I fucking earn it, and they know I'll deal with them accordingly. Hate me all you want, but you know I'm right."

They sat in silence as he drove across the strip, heading toward the hospital where Ned told him to go.

"I just want you to know, it's not a thing, not wanting to go back to The Skulls. I wouldn't blame you if you didn't."

Butch didn't say anything.

****

"Everything is here, wrapped and ready to go." Cheryl smiled at Ned.

He shook his head. "You're too good of a wife."

"I've got nothing better to do." She looked at the gift basket she'd spent the entire day making after Butch told her what happened.

One of his fighters was in the hospital and had been beaten in a pretty bad way. She wanted to help, and seeing as she was forced to stay at home for the most part, she didn't see a reason why she couldn't do this kind gesture.

"You better not be stressing yourself out. I want that baby to come out strong."

She put a hand on her swollen stomach. "We're doing good."

"You spend too much time on your own. I don't like that."

"It's fine. I've never really been good at the whole making friends thing." She tucked some hair behind her ear and watched Ned.

He kept on staring at her.

"What is it?"

"I was just wondering if you're planning on going

back to Fort Wills anytime soon?"

She shook her head. "I don't think so, why?"

"Do you want to go back?" he asked.

She nibbled her lip. When she thought about Fort Wills, it filled her with a sense of unease. "I don't really know."

"Come on, it's not a hard question."

"I don't know if it's something I'll ever be able to do, so it seems kind of pointless even talking about it." She tilted her head to the side. "What are you up to?"

"I'm just wondering. You and Butch, you've been here a while, and something has changed between the two of you."

She touched her stomach. "It's the baby. The nerves."

"I don't think that's all it is. You two need to sit down and actually talk about what you both want from your future."

She snorted. "Yeah, we can't even get in the same room together for long enough to talk about plans for the future. We're kind of waiting to see how this goes."

"And what do you do then? I know from experience having a kid is not easy. You don't have more time to talk. You have less time."

"I know that."

"Does Butch?"

"He's not around all that much, Ned. I can't force him to sit and talk to me."

"Why not?"

"Because, it's bad enough that we can't..." Her cheeks were heating. She was a grown ass woman, and talking to Ned was like talking to her father, or maybe even her grandfather. "You know."

"Have sex?"

"Yeah."

Ned stared at her with a frown.

"What?" she asked.

He was giving her this weird look that was really starting to unnerve her.

"What? Why do you keep looking at me like that?"

"I'm an old man. I've seen a lot of things. Done a lot of good and bad things, but I'm not exactly sure what the hell is going on right now."

She chuckled. "I have no idea what you're talking about."

"You don't want to have physical sex because of the troubles that can cause. I get that. I understand it. Right there with you, but, and here is a pretty big but, you do know that there's a lot more to fucking than just sex, right?"

"You and I really shouldn't be talking about this."

"I'm being serious. You had the talk about the whole sex thing, right?"

"Of course I did. I'm nearly a mother of two." This had to be the weirdest conversation she'd ever had.

"Then you know there's a lot more to fucking than just sex, right? There's that magical word of foreplay, and you can do to each other that doesn't have to go to the full physical. You play with him, he plays with you. You don't have to ignore each other."

"Did you have this conversation with Eva?"

"Nope, and as far as I'm concerned, she's still a virgin who can produce children at will," Ned said. "Have you two seriously gone that long without sex?"

"Ned, I don't think this is an appropriate topic for us to talk about."

"Someone has to, otherwise you're going to dry up. Sex is necessary, and it's damn good and pleasurable. You need to think of a way to bring your man back in.

Talk to him about your plans for the future and don't take no for an answer. He's not fucking anyone at the gym either, so I don't know what his excuse is. You need to get your man in check."

Ned picked up the gift basket, and she waddled her way to the door.

She gave him a wave as he left. Again, he wasn't driving but had someone from the gym take him everywhere.

From what Eva had told her once, her father didn't like to drive if he didn't need to. Closing the door, she rested against it and wondered what to do with that kind of information. It had been a long time since she'd tried to seduce Butch.

Could it work?

The doctor who she visited once a week had told her everything was progressing normally and that she didn't see a reason to worry. Her baby was strong, as was she, and she didn't foresee any complications.

She couldn't help but worry even though her pregnancy had progressed healthily.

Her concerns were because of previous miscarriages.

She and Butch hadn't progressed this long in a pregnancy before.

Ned was right.

She'd been holding everything off for fear of what the future would hold. In doing so, she'd pushed Butch away.

Moving from the door, she made her way upstairs to their bedroom. Staring at herself in the mirror, she winced. She wore a pair of maternity pants and a shirt. The baby bump was in full swing, and it was so big.

She didn't feel sexy, far from it.

She was still able to get about and function. She

could sit and stand, though admittedly, it was getting increasingly difficult now.

"Not much longer to go and you're coming out. I can't wait to meet you, but before then, I'm going to have to be really patient." Opening the closet door, she stepped inside and opened the drawer where she kept her special lingerie. The sexy kind. Lifting them up, she felt her cheeks heat. This could go really badly.

Still, she was willing to do whatever it took to get Butch to talk to her, to spend some time with her, and for them both to stop yelling.

She was the one that did most of the yelling.

She took a quick shower, and wasn't able to actually shave because she couldn't reach her ankles, but she did underneath her arms. She washed her hair, soaped all of her body, and turned the water off when she was done.

Once she was dry, she stepped into the sexy thong and sheer lace panties before adding the wrap that gave her some semblance of modesty. It was not a lot, but it would do for what she wanted. When that was done, she finished her hair, put some makeup on, and headed downstairs to the kitchen.

Putting some beers in the fridge, she grabbed her cell phone and hovered over his name.

She hadn't phoned him at work in so long.

Would he like the interruption?

You're planning a seduction. How can you do that if he doesn't know to come home alone?

Biting her lip, she dialed his number and waited.

"Hello," he said.

He sounded out of breath. She heard several men panting.

"Hey," she said. "It's me."

He chuckled. "I know, babe. I saw your name on

my call ID. Do it again, harder this time."

"What?" she asked.

"Sorry, I was just telling one of the guys how to throw a punch properly. Two seconds, let me get out of here."

She heard all the noise and then the sound of doors opening and closing.

"I saw the gift basket you did for Punk. Thanks, babe. All the boys loved it. We had some things to add to it, but other than that, it was good."

"Why do I feel porno magazines were involved?" she asked.

"That's because they totally were. He's a young kid with a wild imagination."

"You're all bad."

"Just the way you like us."

She giggled.

"What's wrong, babe? It has been a long time since you called me at work."

"It has been too long. There's nothing wrong, really, I just wanted to make sure that you came home tonight, around seven. I've got a surprise for you, and I really need for you to come alone."

"You know I love surprises."

"Well, I hope you'll love this one."

"Sounds promising. I'll be home by seven, promise."

She couldn't stop smiling. "I love you, Butch."

"I love you too, baby, always. Never forget that."

He hung up, and she stared at the phone.

She could handle this.

Chapter Four

As he sat in his driveway at six-fifty-six, anticipation filled Butch in every single fiber of his being. He wanted nothing more than to enter his home and for everything to be fine.

The way Cheryl had spoken to him on the phone made him think of sex, of need, of everything he wanted to do to her and then some. Would it be so wrong to pull out of the driveway right now, and call her to say something had come up?

He shook his head.

"You're not a coward, Butch. Get out of the fucking car."

Climbing out of the car, he didn't look back as he clicked the lock and made his way into his home. The scent of citrus fruits filled the air, and he noticed candles lit his way. Closing the door, he was careful not to blow out any of the candles because he saw she'd worked so hard.

His heart raced as he followed the path of candles. When he came to the sitting room, he saw his wife, curled up on the sofa, smiling at him. Her hair was curled around her face, and she wore the red lingerie that he knew she'd bought but he'd never seen—and his cock went from flaccid to hard within seconds.

"Hey, handsome," she said.

He watched as she climbed off the sofa.

She struggled a little, but she didn't ask for his help. He stepped up to her, and she placed her hands on his chest.

"Hey, baby. What's all this?" he asked.

"Do you like it?"

"I do."

"Then don't think." She went onto her tiptoes,

using his body to help steady her as her lips brushed against his. Her stomach touched his body, and he cupped her hips, holding her close.

She released a moan, and he curved his hand down to cup her ass. It had been too long since he'd touched his wife, since he'd felt her fill his hands, and he was hard for her once again.

He wanted to do nothing more than spread her on the floor and fuck her.

That wasn't going to happen though.

"What's going on, Cheryl?" he asked.

"I want to make love to my husband."

"We can't."

She nibbled his lip, making him moan. "Yes, we can. If I tell you a certain man told me there was more to fucking than just sex, what would you say?"

"Who the fuck have you been talking to?"

"Ned Walker."

He knew Ned picked up the gift basket. "You were talking about our sex lives with Ned?"

"*I* wasn't talking about it. It came up—anyway, he was saying how there's more things for us to try, and I figured seeing as we'd not even given them a try, I want to." She ran her hands down his chest, to his dick.

The instant her hand touched his length, he was in such a happy place. Even through the jeans, that touch was more than enough.

"What do you think, Butch? I don't want to lose you, and I know that if we're not careful, we're going to lose each other. I can feel you slipping away. I can't stand it. I love you more than anything else in the world."

"You're not going to lose me, baby. We don't have to do this. We can wait."

"For what? I need you." She began to tug on his belt and moving him back so that he sat on the sofa.

CHRISTMAS COMES BUTCH ONCE A YEAR

He didn't fight her. The truth was he didn't want to fight her.

He grabbed her hand and tugged her down onto his lap so that she was straddling him. Her stomach was a constant reminder of the night he fucked her, of when he finally got her pregnant.

Running his hands down her back, he gripped her ass, and she kissed him. He kept one hand at her ass, and the other he sank into the locks of hair.

"I've missed this," she said.

"Babe, this is what has been driving me crazy. I fucking love you, and this for me, this is what I've been wanting for a long time." He pulled her down and kissed her lips. The little moan she gave went straight to his cock.

"I wish you could fuck me. I want you to take me."

"Soon, babe."

"I know. I know. I didn't think you wanted me anymore."

He slid his hand from her butt to her inner thigh, caressing up until he found her wet slit. "You're so wet. Never doubt that I want you. You drive me crazy with need. All I can think about is fucking you, being with you. The only reason I stayed away was because I thought you'd want that."

She whimpered as he stroked across her clit. "Never. I don't want to lose you. You're mine, Butch." She kissed down his neck, sucking on his pulse. "I want to make you feel good."

He watched and helped her as she sank to the floor in front of him.

Her tongue peeked out, running across her lip, and it made him ache to feel those lips around his dick.

She reached out, grabbing his zipper and sliding it

down.

He took over, gripping his cock, running his hand up and down the length. The tip was already leaking copious amounts of pre-cum.

He'd been pleasuring himself in the shower whenever the need arose, but he wasn't going to take that satisfaction anymore.

"Every time I touched myself, I thought of you."

She covered his cock with her hand, and he showed her exactly what he wanted and how he liked it. When she licked the tip of his dick, and he watched her taste him, he was close to coming just then.

"This is not going to last," he said.

"Good. I don't want it to last. I want to blow your mind, Butch." With that, she covered the head of his cock and started to take him deep into her mouth.

He moaned as her mouth moved down on his length, sucking him in until he hit the back of her throat. She took her time working him, running her tongue up and down the length until she had him wanting more. Her lips teased him, made him ache. His balls tightened.

"It has been too long since I did this," she said, lifting up off his dick long enough to talk. He watched her swirl her tongue around the head before down she went, coating all of his dick in her saliva.

She bobbed her head up and down his length, and he tried to think of everything and anything that could stop him from exploding.

It was no good though.

The pleasure of her mouth, feeling her tightening lips around him, he needed it, and as he filled her mouth, she swallowed every single drop, milking him of his cum.

When it was over, he lifted her up, and not caring that she had his taste on her tongue, he kissed her.

CHRISTMAS COMES BUTCH ONCE A YEAR

"My turn." Placing her on the sofa, he got to his feet and got rid of his clothes. He didn't need them.

She laughed, and the sound was sweet music to him.

"I love watching you get naked. All of your ink on display."

"You should know that after that, I'm not letting you go. Not even for a second. You belong to me, and I'm going to make sure you know it, even if I can't fuck you." Kissing her lips, he started to trail them down her neck, sucking on her pulse.

The robe she wore opened up, and he caught sight of her body in the sexy lingerie. Opening the straps, he revealed her pregnant self.

Her stomach was so large, carrying their child, her tits full and ripe, getting ready to feed their kid.

When he looked at her, he saw sheer perfection.

Sliding his hands up, he cupped her tits, pressing them together. He licked across each beaded nipple, tasting her.

"Hello, ladies, I know it has been a long time since I tasted you. I know, she has kept you away from me."

"Are you seriously talking to my breasts right now?" she asked, giggling.

"Of course. We need to become acquainted once again. I'm not going to take advantage." Sucking one nipple into his mouth, he relished the sounds she made as he showed her body exactly how much he'd been missing her.

When he got that call today, he knew she was planning something, but he just didn't have a clue exactly what. He'd hoped to fix this rift between them that hadn't even been intentionally caused.

He hated fighting with her.

She was his woman, and he'd move heaven and earth to make her happy. He only hoped that what he wanted would make her so.

****

Cheryl watched as he teased her nipples.

She couldn't believe it had been eight months since they'd been together, since they'd been this intimate.

Getting pregnant hadn't been a need or anything like that. They wanted children, but it had become something it didn't have to be, and in doing so, they'd lost themselves.

She sent a quick thank you in her head to Ned and made a note to thank him when she saw him. Butch bit down on her nipples, and she screamed his name, not wanting him to stop as he soothed the pain with his tongue.

She felt on fire with need. He was driving her wild.

"Please, Butch," she said.

"You want my tongue on your pussy."

"Yes."

"Good. You're going to get it." He continued to torture her nipples though, and even though she loved it, it was not where she wanted him.

Whimpering, she screamed his name, and he finally started to kiss down her stomach.

"Now, I don't know if you can see or hear anything, but close your eyes and think about something else."

"Butch, stop it," she said, laughing.

"I'm just checking. Our child is so clever."

She watched him caress her stomach, and then he was between her thighs. He lifted her legs so one rested on his shoulder and the other on the floor. He grabbed a pillow, moving it beneath her ass to help spread her open.

"There we go. You have such a pretty pussy. I imagine this would win awards."

"Please stop."

He licked through her slit, and she cried out. He circled her clit before sucking it into his mouth.

She hadn't wanted to give herself a climax. The doctor had given her so many books, and she saw orgasms wouldn't be helpful to her. Since she was close to the final weeks, her doctor had said she was out of the danger zone and they were looking at having a good pregnancy. All the precautions had paid off. As he started to stroke through her slit, his fingers moving inside her, pumping within her, she couldn't believe how close she came to release, and when he flicked her clit, back and forth twice and she came, she did so hard.

Covering her face with her hands, she couldn't believe that within five minutes of his expert touch, she'd come.

He kissed her leg. "I've been a bad husband."

"No, you haven't. You're been patient with me. I've been a bitch."

"I love you, Cheryl."

"I can't believe I came so quickly." She sniffled, feeling emotional all of a sudden.

He moved up, making sure not to squash her, giving her plenty of space. "My tongue is the best one around, you know that. The moment I touched you, it was over."

She chuckled and turned toward him. Cupping his cheek, she stroked her thumb back and forth. A day's worth of stubble already covered his face. She didn't mind. To her, it just made him look more handsome.

"I don't want to lose you again."

"You won't. We lost ourselves there for a moment, but we've got it back." He kissed her inner wrist. "I'm never losing you, baby. You have to understand that. You, me, our baby, and Michael. We're all a family."

"Michael. I miss him."

"I miss him too. The temper tantrum little bastard."

This made her laugh again.

"I want to take you out tomorrow," he said.

"You do?"

"Yes, I want to take you to dinner. I know you can't do much in the way of walking. I've got work in the morning, but after that, are you clear all day?"

"I have such a busy schedule," she said, rolling her eyes. "Watching television, walking to the kitchen, you know, stuff like that."

"Sounds like a lot to do for a pregnant woman."

"It is, but I think I can squeeze you in."

"Good, wear something nice."

"I don't think it matters what I wear, I'll still look pregnant."

"And it's a good look on you." He gripped the back of her neck, kissing her hard. "How about we try again and see if you can last ten minutes?"

She couldn't help but take his challenge. After all, they had a lot to catch up on.

Chapter Five

Whistling, Butch placed out the towels as Javier, Mistletoe, and Cruz watched him. He felt their gazes on him as if he was some kind of foreign object.

"You're in a good mood," Javier said.

"Of course he is. His wife took my advice," Ned said, coming out of the office.

"You stay away from my wife. She's all mine."

"I miss seeing Cheryl around," Javier said. "She always kept everyone in a good mood."

"You shouldn't start fights, and then she'd be able to come around a lot more." Butch hummed as he picked up an empty bottle off the floor. The fighters weren't due to arrive until after twelve, and the morning gym was given to the civilians who just wanted to work out. This was a front for Ned's fighting business. All of the cops knew what he did, but he kept them in money to keep them out of his business.

"It's impossible not to start a fight. Half of the guys here want to be hit," Mistletoe said.

"So you got some last night. Got some pregnant pussy?" Cruz asked.

"You're just nasty," Javier said.

"What? You not heard how horny pregnant ladies are? They are begging for the cock, and if they want it, I'm more than willing to give it to them."

Butch shook his head.

"I need you down at the hospital," Ned said.

"Why?"

"Punk is trying to sign out, and he can't leave yet."

"Why not?" Butch asked.

"They need to keep him in for observation to make sure nothing gets worse. Will you do the honors and check on him?"

"Will do." He hummed to himself as he left the gym.

He pulled his car keys out of his pocket. There were times like this that he missed his bike. When he first got to Vegas, he owned three different bikes, and each had been stolen. He was sure Ned had something to do with it, but rather than argue with the miserable old bastard, he decided to get a car.

Since then, his car hadn't been stolen. He could probably get a bike now. He owned a house with a garage, but seeing as he was out of the house so often, he didn't want to put Cheryl at risk.

He was a paranoid sort.

Still humming to himself, he opened the car door and stopped at his name being called.

Javier had followed him outside.

"Hold up," Javier said.

"You want to go and pay Punk a visit?"

"Nah, I'm good. I wanted to talk to you."

"What about?"

"You know what about. Have you given it some thought?" Javier asked.

Butch rubbed at his chin. "It's not my call."

"You're not going home. You know that, I know it. Why can't you just accept that it's time to move on?"

"You're asking me to throw my club away. I can't do that."

"Why are you still loyal to them?" Javier asked. "I get that you had to be punished, but when is enough enough?"

"Look, this is not your call. It's not my call."

"So you're just going to head back to Fort Wills when they finally decide to get their heads out of their asses?"

"This is why you'll never be good enough to join the MC. You need to learn to deal with the hierarchy of the club. I do as I'm told to do."

"No, you're sitting around rather than face reality. You're as good as any Prez. I've met my fair share of them. I'm not some civilian here, Butch. You have what it takes to be a leader."

"I'm not talking about this now."

"You've thought about it though."

He let out a breath and stared at his friend. Javier, Mistletoe, and Cruz had told him over the years that they would be willing to join any extension of an MC so long as he was Prez. When he told Cheryl about their idea, she thought it was a good one, and one he should have spoken to Lash about. He never brought it up, even though he'd wanted to. Lash was a good guy, and they'd talked plenty on the phone.

"Look, I think it's a good idea, okay? Starting a brand-new MC is not what I want to do. The Skulls know their shit. I'm a brother there, and I'm not going to turn my back on them."

"We're not asking you to turn your back but to show them you can create a chapter right here. That's what I'm suggesting. You got to stop acting like you've got to stay punished. You've done your time, paid your dues, and showed your loyalty. We've got your back, Butch. Just like you've had ours all these years." Javier sighed. "See you around."

He watched as Javier headed back into the gym.

Ned had brought up something similar a few months ago. Like always, Butch put off the topic of conversation.

Pulling out his cell phone, he stared at Lash's number, and he was so tempted to dial.

Only he stopped himself, pocketed his cell,

climbed behind the wheel, and headed back to the hospital.

The drive this time didn't take him as long. When he arrived, he parked as far away from the door as possible and walked the short distance. He needed the time to clear his head.

He never liked hospitals. Nothing good ever came from being near them. As far as he was concerned, too many people died in them.

When he entered the hospital, no one stopped him as he made his way to Punk's room. The nurse was on the way out as he entered.

"Are you family?" she asked.

"A friend."

"Oh, well, we had an incident, and we had to call security."

As she talked, Butch looked past her shoulder to see Punk was in fact cuffed to the bed.

"It's fine. I won't let him out."

"We don't want him causing any more trouble."

"He won't."

He walked past the woman and sat down on the chair beside Punk's bed.

Punk still hadn't talked, and Butch wasn't about to make the first move. The kid was full of aggression and rage.

"I don't want you here," Punk said.

"Ned sent me to talk some sense into you."

"Sent you? You're the reason I can't help my mom. Why did you have to go and stick your nose where it don't belong? My life doesn't concern you."

"True."

"You're an asshole." Punk pulled on his arm, but it was useless.

"I'm sorry about your mom."

Punk snorted. "What the fuck do you care? The money I was earning was to take care of her. To pay for *her* medical bills. Not mine. This is just fucking … you know what, I don't fucking need this. I got to fight that Christmas fight. You've got to let me."

"It's not going to happen."

"Why? What makes you boss? I thought the infamous Ned Walker made all the decisions."

Butch smiled. There was a time he was exactly like this kid. Especially the young part and thinking he was invincible. It took a few smackdowns to learn the truth, that was for sure.

"What the fuck you smirking at? You think this is funny?"

"I'm not laughing at you."

"I fucking hate you and everything you stand for." Punk rattled his arm again, and Butch saw the fight drain right out of him.

"Are you done now? Do you think I can talk?"

"Sure, go ahead and talk. Doesn't mean I'm going to listen."

Butch listened to the silence that filled the room. The buzzing of the hospital staff outside the door. The calm.

"I hate hospitals."

"Yeah, well, welcome to the fucking club."

"You sure like the word fuck."

"It's my word, deal with it, fuckhead."

Again, Butch smiled. He wondered if Michael was turning out this way for Alex.

Damn, he missed that kid.

Making the decision for him to head back to Fort Wills had been hard. Between work and Cheryl, and Michael's sucky attitude, he didn't have a choice.

Yeah, Michael had been a pain in the ass.

Who wasn't at that age?

Still, being around Punk reminded him of that.

"You can't fight because you'll die and then what will your mom do?" Butch asked.

"I'm not going to die. I'm stronger than I look."

"You know, I've met men stronger than you. They've been prepared, knew the risks, and yet they still fucking died. You think this is a game. A fight and if you get knocked out, that's it. You've got to put on a show, a performance, and there's a good chance someone will die. It's the way it is. Ned Walker does fights where the odds are all over the place. I get that you think you're ready, but look at what you did now. You're in the hospital, and you're not getting out for some time. You're not ready. You think I want to put men in that ring for them to die? Let me tell you something, I've been around death a hell of a long time. I've watched good men and women die. It's the way of the world, but each time someone close to you goes, it fucks with your head. You lose a part of yourself. Your mother, you're all she has left. You die in that ring, you're signing her death sentence."

Punk's eyes glistened with unshed tears. "It's what I've got to do," Punk said.

"No, it's not. You can find the money another way. Constantly pay every single month. You don't need to kill yourself to fix your mom, because here's another thing—if you die for this, your mother isn't going to want the money."

Butch sat back in his chair, allowing that piece of information to sink in.

He knew it did because Punk stopped fighting with the damn cuffs.

Seconds passed.

Then minutes.

"She's all I've got," Punk said. "I know it's not cool, but she's my mom and I'll do anything for her."

"I've not told you to not do anything for her. I've told you to think about her and what your idea of paying her fees will do to her. You're not being selfish."

The tears finally started to fall then, and as he fell apart, sobbing, Butch moved to the bed, grabbed the kid's hand, and offered him some support.

"I don't want her to die."

"I know."

"I can't do this without her. I don't have anything to offer. Fighting is all I know. I don't..."

"Don't think right now. Just focus and you'll come up with something." He stayed there for the rest of the day, giving the kid some company, and he hoped by the time he left, that he'd gotten through to him.

Death was hard.

Ned Walker had lost a lot of men in his fighting rings. Butch had seen the effects it had on the older man. He tried to hide it, but it was there. The pain of the loss was a part of him.

Ned didn't breed losers.

It's why he worked so damn hard to get the fighters strong.

Death wasn't going to get a helping hand from either of them.

****

One week later

Cheryl stared up at the café she'd been asked to visit. Putting a hand on her stomach, she thought about the morning she'd spent with Butch before he headed to the hospital. Punk was due to be released in another week. The beating he'd taken was pretty serious, and there had been some fear of internal bleeding.

Poor kid.

Fortunately, he seemed to be making a full recovery, and she was a day closer to her due date, and that was a good thing. Her baby also liked to make her or his presence known with the constant kicking, but she wasn't going to complain about that. She loved feeling this baby inside her, and since talking with Butch, life felt ... good. Less complicated, at least.

She knew there was still a lot of work to be done for her and for Butch, but in time they could work on that.

She wasn't going to give up on them or this relationship. Keep moving forward, that was her motto right now.

Pushing some hair behind her ear, she released a breath and decided to just head on inside.

Opening the door, she saw it was busy, and scanning the crowd, she found Alex pretty damn easily. He sat in a private booth facing the door.

He'd told her where he'd be.

She saw no one else was with him. Sunshine, his wife, she adored.

Walking past the tables, she took her time, careful as she walked. The doctor had told her that any serious fall, and she'd need to go to the hospital right away. With every single passing day, Butch had been firm in his decision to only hire the best doctors.

Taking a seat in the booth, she removed her jacket and offered Alex a smile.

There was a time she'd hated this man sitting across from her.

He was a manipulative bastard, but of course she was biased, seeing as he'd left her with a kid, and not even his name.

"Hey, Alex," she said.

"How are you doing, Cheryl?" he asked.

"I'm doing good." She tucked her hair behind her ears and waited.

He signaled to the waitress and made sure to order her favorite. It wasn't coffee, she couldn't have that, but the blend of tea was her favorite.

"You remembered."

"I remember a lot of things. Being a businessman, it helps me to remember."

"Yes, who could forget? How is business and Sunshine?"

"The hotel is doing wonderfully, as always. The casino as well. Between Sunshine and my kids, life is good. Sunshine is everything to me. I've left her back home. She didn't need to come on this trip, and Vegas doesn't really suit her."

"How is Michael?"

"I brought him along for the trip. He's stopped by Ned's first. I hope that's okay."

"Oh, does he even want to see me?" She nibbled her lip.

Before Michael had left to go and be with his father, they'd argued. He'd accused her of loving the new unborn baby more than him, and of course a lot of other accusations had flown around. They'd hurt, no doubt about it.

Putting a hand to her stomach, she waited.

"He misses you, Cheryl. Don't doubt that for a second."

"I don't doubt it. I just ... I don't want him to think it was an easy decision for me to make."

"How is the pregnancy?"

"It's doing good. I think. I hope. I mean..." She put a hand to her stomach. "Yeah, we're still going strong."

"You look amazing."

"I do?"

"Yes, really healthy, and you're smiling as well. The stress the last time I saw you was clearly getting to you. It's good to see you're doing well, and if I can say it, it's a good look on you."

"Thanks."

"How are things with Butch?"

"We're doing good, I think, for the most part. It has been stressful with this, and I don't even know why I'm talking to you about my relationship with another man, or that we're even being able to have this conversation right now. It's kind of surreal."

"That's true." Alex chuckled. "You know, I never really hated you."

"I find that hard to believe."

"That was a … trying time, don't you think? The stress. The expectation. It was all the pressure, built up in one, and I didn't handle it very well," Alex said.

"Neither of us did. We had the loves of our lives, and it all went to shit." She stared down at her hands. "We can't keep living in the past though."

She stopped as the waitress brought her tea and her favorite muffin. Saying her thanks, she stared down at the offering and felt overwhelmed with emotion.

"You're going to cry, aren't you?"

"I'm sorry. I'm just really emotional. Everything seems to be piling on me all of a sudden."

"Is that why you wanted to see me?" Alex asked. "I was shocked by your call."

She'd reached out to Alex. They'd not had the best relationship out of all of The Skulls, but they had the one connection neither of them could deny: their son, Michael.

"I wanted to talk to you about Butch, about The Skulls, about a lot of things."

"Michael has told me before we came over here that he doesn't want to stay," Alex said. "I'm not saying this to be a bastard, but I'm letting you know."

Tears filled her eyes, but she smiled. She still saw a lot of Michael, and they did talk regularly.

"He wants to be with his dad, and I can't blame him for that." She released a breath. "I'm not upset or angry."

"He doesn't want to upset you. That's why he asked me to double-check that you're okay with him staying with me."

"Of course. I know he's in really good hands with you."

Alex nodded. "I will protect him always. I love him. You and I, we don't always see eye to eye, but I think the one good thing we ever did was make that kid."

"Then we can agree on something." She released a breath. "I think this is a world record for us. Look at how we're talking and there's no flames. We must be growing up."

He laughed. "It had to happen eventually."

She knew she couldn't put it off any longer. "Butch."

"What about him?"

"Do you know if Lash is going to call him back to Fort Wills?"

Alex stared at her. "I don't make those decisions anymore. I helped Tiny out, but that is all on Lash, and I have to say, the kid knows what he's doing."

"You don't know at all?"

"Do you want to come back home?"

She felt a twinge in her chest. Fort Wills wasn't home.

Even though settling down here with Ned Walker for company had been hard to do, she'd gotten used to it.

This was home now, and part of her was afraid that Butch wanted to go back to Fort Wills.

She didn't know if he'd be able to handle that life though.

The life of being a Skull.

In the years they'd been together, so much had happened between them. She'd seen the leader inside him flourish, especially with Ned for company. There was no way a leader could deny his place with that man there. He brought out the best in people. She'd seen it. Not many people liked him, or at least, the men he pissed off didn't like him.

He was a good man.

He hid it well.

"I don't know."

"I don't know the answers you want, Cheryl. Honestly, I'm a Skull, but I don't play as a big a part in that life anymore." He reached across the table and took her hands. "If you want me to talk to Lash, I will."

"You'd do that?"

"Of course."

She squeezed his hands. "I don't think I want to go back to Fort Wills. I think our life is here."

"Okay."

"But I don't think Butch being a Skull in the capacity he is, is enough anymore."

"You think he wants more."

"I think he deserves it." She shrugged. "I don't know. Everything is so confusing right now, and I know I'm not making any sense."

"I've got some advice though. You want to hear it?"

"Please."

"Talk to your husband. It's a great deciding factor when you want to get a job done."

She couldn't help it; she burst out laughing. "Wow, I can't believe we're doing this. Talking, having a conversation. It's really crazy."

"Second time, I know." He was laughing though. "We've come a long way."

"I need to use the bathroom," she said.

Climbing out of the stall, she took a step and felt wetness on her feet.

Glancing down, she saw it looked like she'd wet herself, only she knew that wasn't the case.

"Holy shit, is that, has your water broken?"

"Yes, I need to go to the hospital."

Staff were already rushing to her, and as she gripped her stomach, a contraction hit her hard.

"It's too soon. It's way too soon. Shouldn't we be forty weeks? It's too soon."

"Come on. I'll get you to the hospital, and then get Butch."

Chapter Six

Butch burst through the hospital doors. He went to the main desk, got the directions he needed, and took off. He followed all the signs, and as he threw open the doors, he came to a stop as he caught sight of Alex and Michael. He'd left Ned and the others behind.

Ned offered to drive him.

As if he'd trust that old fool to get him to the hospital in one piece.

"Where is she?" Butch asked. He was panting for breath as he looked at Alex.

"She's in the delivery room." Alex walked past him to the counter.

Butch ran a hand down his face, his heart racing.

They'd planned this for the past couple of weeks, how it would go down. They'd even done some practice runs so he didn't panic in getting her to the hospital. Only right now, he was panicking.

"Cheryl, my wife, I need to go and see her."

"I'm sorry, sir, but that's not possible."

"She's in labor, and she needs me by her side. At least tell the doctor who is handling her care that I'm here." He gave the doctor's name while Alex tried to negotiate with the women to get him into the damn room.

One of the women took off with his details, and he stood, waiting.

"Was she okay? Did she seem okay? Was she in a lot of pain?"

"She was in a lot of pain with the contractions. Her water broke in the café that we were eating in, and she seemed fine. More than fine. She looked healthy."

He nodded. "She's fine. She's going to be fine."

"Yes, she is. Believe me, she looked ready for this." Alex put a hand on his shoulder. "She's going to get through this."

He nodded. Pacing the length of the floor, he saw that Michael was staring at him.

He walked over to the kid and smiled. "You still want to punch me in the face? Last time you saw me you said you were going to put me on my ass."

"You said that?" Alex asked, taking a seat beside his kid.

"Yeah." Michael's face was red.

"It's a good thing it was your stepfather you threatened and not a grown-ass man who'd put you on the floor," Alex said.

"You teaching him some manners while he's with you?" Butch asked.

"I'm sitting right here," Michael said.

"Exactly, and as a good young man, you'll take it."

"I don't have to sit and listen to this," Michael said.

"Sit your ass down. You think about causing me any trouble, and you'll have your allowance cut and your privileges removed," Alex said.

"Adulting sucks, right?" Butch asked.

"I don't remember being this big a pain in the ass. I wonder where he gets it from."

Michael folded his arms and slumped down in his seat as if the weight of the world was on his singular shoulders.

Butch saw the truth though. The kid, with all his attitude, was worried about his mom, and it was making him lash out.

"She'll be okay."

"You don't know that," Michael said.

The doors opened, and a nurse was waiting. "Cheryl's waiting for you, Butch."

Taking off, he didn't look back at Alex and Michael. He needed to see his woman.

The nurse made him quickly put a gown on to cover his clothes, and he had to wash his hands.

Once that was done, he entered a room, and there was his wife, on the table, legs spread, and she looked in pain.

"You're doing so good, Cheryl. Look, your husband is here right now."

"He did this to me," she said, whimpering.

He smiled. The doctor had told him when the pregnancy started that during the birth, the man is responsible for everything. The woman is always the victim.

"If my memory serves me well, Cheryl, you loved every second of it." Butch said, moving behind her and taking her hands.

He'd dreamed of this moment and dreaded it with equal measure.

He'd been warned of the dangers of pregnancy, and it scared him to think of his wife going through this.

Holding her hands tightly, he tried to offer her the support she needed.

"It hurts," she said, crying out.

"I know. I know. Come on, baby. Another push, and you're almost there."

"I tried to wait for you," Cheryl said.

"I'm here now. Alex called me immediately. Don't worry. I'm here, and I love you. Come on, baby. One more push. I'm right here. Your pain is my pain. Come on."

Cheryl lifted up, and he saw she was exhausted.

"One. Two. Three. Push."

She pushed with all of her might, and she still had some strength in her. She held his hands as she screamed out her pain, and he took every single second of it.

Each scream and clench of her hand, and then he heard it.

The sound of the newborn baby.

His child.

His son or daughter.

Cheryl collapsed against him, and he watched as the doctors and nurses got to work.

"Butch, what's happening? I want to see my baby. Is everything okay?"

He saw the fear in her eyes, and he saw the doctors doing their work. They'd been told the process, and as their doctor turned toward them, he waited, and finally, after what felt like a lifetime, he smiled.

"You have a beautiful, healthy baby girl."

Butch watched as the doctor brought their baby girl toward them, and as he laid her down on Cheryl's chest, Butch saw his little girl.

"Look what we did."

He reached out, putting his fingers beneath her hand and marveled at how tiny she was. She gripped his finger and let out a little baby noise, opening her eyes.

"She's so pretty," he said. Kissing Cheryl's head, he couldn't believe that he was finally a dad.

Sharing in this moment, he felt all the love consume him, for his wife, for his child, for the life they'd built together.

What they'd gone through these past months, for this moment, he'd never forget, and it had been so worth it.

There was no other feeling in the world that could ever replace this one. His love was so damn strong.

He stayed by Cheryl's side, and as she was being processed to go to another room, just for observation as she'd struggled to take a baby to term previously, he took his daughter in his arms.

"Am I okay to take her out? To show her to her brother?" Butch asked.

The nurse nodded. "Of course. Make sure you support her head."

"I will."

He was going to protect this girl for his entire life.

He walked out of the hospital room. He expected to only see Alex and Michael, but Ned had arrived, as well as several fighters. Javier, Mistletoe, and Cruz were waiting for him as well.

They were all there to show their love and support.

"I have a beautiful baby girl," he said.

Ned was the first to approach. "How is Cheryl?"

"She's doing well. They're just going to get her settled into a room, and then I'll go back with her."

The men each took a turn to come and see her, and then he went to Michael. Sitting down in the available seat, he smiled.

"Hey, sweetheart, this is your big brother. He has attitude, but I think one day he's going to see what an amazing man he's turning into and he'll protect you. He acts all hard, but he's really a big marshmallow."

"I'm sitting right here."

"That I know. Look at her, Michael. Don't be a pain in the ass."

Michael turned his head, and he waited. "She's so small."

"She is. She's going to need a big brother someday."

"I'll be around," Michael said. "Can I see my mom?"

"Of course. Come on."

He made sure to look to Alex, who gave him a

nod.

Michael followed him back toward Cheryl's room, and there his wife sat, looking so damn exhausted and cute.

She smiled at him, and as he moved out of the way, he saw the joy on her face at Michael. She held open her arms, and her son went right into them.

"You're getting so big. It's illegal for you to get any taller. What are they feeding you?"

Michael laughed. "Food, Mom, just good food."

"Well, I'll just have to deal with you being a lot taller than me."

****

Cheryl didn't have anything wrong with her. The doctor had said to her that the body was a beautiful and mysterious thing. No one knew why she'd suffered the miscarriages before while this pregnancy went by without a single hitch. Either way, she loved it.

Lying down in the sitting room, she stared at her baby, who was wriggling beside her.

"We need to think of a name," Butch said.

He lay on the other side of their little girl.

Alex and Michael had gone back to Fort Wills. She'd been able to spend a couple of days with her son, but for the most part, it had been in the hospital. The doctor wasn't going to take any risks with her health, and she had a feeling that was down to Butch. He was pretty scary when he wanted to be.

"I know. What about Anna?" she asked.

"Nah, it doesn't suit her."

"Elizabeth."

"Lexie and Devil's kid is called that."

She laughed. "They have so many kids, they probably have all the good names."

"That's true."

"Are you happy?" she asked.

"More than happy." Butch cupped her cheek, their baby between them. "I've got you. That's always been more than enough for me."

She turned toward his open palm and kissed him. "I love you with all my heart."

"You own me."

"I love it when you say that."

Their daughter gurgled, and the sound filled her with even more love. "She is just so perfect."

"You know I'm going to get arrested right? I'm going to have to fight all the guys that want to date her."

"You're going to be old, and don't worry, I'll handle everything. She is going to break some hearts, that's for sure."

She ran her hand down her baby's body, touching her toes.

For so long she'd been worried that her baby wouldn't make it.

Right now, it was kind of surreal that not only had she made it, but she was just so perfect. Every parent went through this. She'd felt the same way with Michael.

"You're a beautiful little girl." Cheryl chuckled. "I keep saying the same thing."

"I know. We still need to pick out a name. Susan."

"Nah, what about Carla?" Cheryl wrinkled her nose. "That doesn't suit her either."

They continued to throw out girls' names, and each one just didn't suit her until Butch finally called one.

"Jade."

Staring at her little girl, Cheryl lifted up and smiled. "Hello, Jade."

"It suits her."

"It really does. Our baby girl is called Jade. I can't believe it." She held Butch's hand as she stared down at their daughter.

"Come on, I think our Jade needs to go to sleep." Butch got to his feet and carefully lifted Jade up in his arms.

There was no better sight than seeing the man she loved cradling their little girl.

She followed him up to the nursery. Standing beside the crib that they'd assembled just hours before, he gently placed their little girl down.

Jade had started to fall asleep downstairs, and now as they turned the light down and watched, she fell asleep completely.

Cheryl moved to Butch's side, taking his hand.

They were a family.

The three of them.

All together.

Resting her head against his arm, she knew that even as she wanted to pause this moment, it wasn't going to happen. They had to make some decisions.

Pulling Butch from the room, she got the baby monitor and they headed downstairs to the kitchen.

She grabbed the ingredients to make the hot chocolate, tension in the air.

"Alex told me you were talking about Fort Wills when your water broke," Butch said.

"Wow, that didn't take long."

"I need to know if you're wanting to head back there," Butch said.

She put the milk in the saucepan and placed it on the stove to start heating. Turning back to face the man she loved, she gripped her shoulders.

"I don't know."

"If you want to go back there, we can."

She stared at him. The wall that Butch put in place to protect himself was very much there. She found it a lot harder to read him when he was like this.

"Tell me what you want," she said.

"It doesn't matter what I want."

"Bullshit. It matters to me." She ran fingers through her hair. "I don't want us to go on this merry-go-round, Butch. Just tell me what it is you want."

"I want you. That's all I want."

"But where exactly do you want me?"

"Wherever you want to be."

She laughed. "All of your life you've done everything that everyone else has ever asked of you without complaint. I'm asking you as your wife, as the woman who loves you, what exactly it is that you want, and you're not being honest with me."

"I don't know what you want me to say, Cheryl."

"What are you thinking? What are you feeling? Do you want to go back to Fort Wills? Do you want to stay here? What is it you want to do? Why can't you be honest?"

"Because I don't want to be selfish. For a long time, Fort Wills was my home, but it's not where I want to be. But I'm not willing to put yours and Jade's happiness on hold for something I want."

"You want to stay here?"

"Yes. I like it here. I've made a life here. *We've* made a life here, and I happen to like Ned, meddling old bastard that he is. He's something else. I love being here, and I can't go back, not now. We can't go back, Cheryl." He'd stood up, and she watched as he closed his eyes, the fight leaving him.

"You don't have to hide who you are from me. You're not this passive person you claim." She took a step toward him. "Don't hold back. Tell me what you want?"

She watched and waited. He didn't say anything for the longest time.

"Your milk is burning."

She turned back to the stove to see the milk boiling over the edge of the saucepan. "Shoot!" She quickly pulled the pan off the stove and cursed. Looking at the spilling, she turned the stove off and then pressed a hand to her forehead.

Butch moved up behind her, wrapping his arms around her waist. "I want to make you happy."

"That's a copout, Butch. For once in your life be honest with me and trust me to have your best interests at heart. Is that too much to ask?" She turned in his arms, cupping his face. "Tell me what it is you want."

Silence fell between them. She held her breath as he continued to stare at her.

Finally, after what felt like a lifetime, he started to talk.

"I don't want to go back to Fort Wills. It's not where our home is, and a couple of the guys have talked to me about us starting a club here, as a charter."

"Like the Vegas chapter or something?" she asked.

"Yes."

"That's good, right?"

"It all depends if Lash wants to expand."

"Have you spoken to him about it?"

"No, the guys have had a lot on their plate."

"So? This is your future like everyone else. Why can't you, I don't know, bring it up to him?"

"I will. When the time is right."

"Do you think you can be a Prez, is that what you call it?" she asked.

"I think I've got what it takes. Yeah. Do you

think you can handle being my old lady?"

"Butch, I threw my body over yours and threatened your entire club to get them to help you. I will do whatever it takes to help you, to be by your side, to love you."

"What about Fort Wills?" he asked.

"What about it?"

"It's your dream."

"Since when? If Fort Wills was my dream, we wouldn't have ever left it. I didn't want to stick around that town. I had you." She went up onto her toes and kissed his lips. "We took our punishment. You've done your time, and you need to stop wearing it like a damn noose around your neck. If Lash has any sense, he'd see what good it would be to have you here with Ned, keeping an eye on things. Especially with it all getting a little messy for them."

He sighed. "There are times you speak a whole lot of sense."

"This is one of those times. Come on, Butch, step out of that darkness you seem to enjoy being in. We made it. We have a beautiful daughter. Michael is flourishing with Alex."

"He told me you two even managed to have a full-blown conversation, you and Alex I mean, without arguing."

"It's called adulting. It's so hard." She rolled her eyes, pretending to hate it. "We've got this."

Butch lowered his mouth against hers and kissed her.

No matter what happened, no matter what they faced, she'd do it, by his side, for the rest of their lives.

Chapter Seven

"You're sure you're okay?" Butch asked.

"Yes. Go. Have fun. Do what you want to do. I'm fine." Cheryl pushed him toward the door.

"You won't put up the tree without me?" Butch asked.

"I'm starting to think he doesn't want to go out and celebrate becoming a dad," Javier said.

Cheryl laughed, but Butch caught her to him, kissing her deeply.

"I don't want to go, but I have to. I've got to go and do the manly thing," he said. The guys had come to his home with Ned in tow. Ned would be sticking around to keep an eye on Cheryl and Jade while Butch went out and celebrated the birth of his baby.

It didn't feel right to him.

"You should be out with me," he said.

"Hey, don't worry about that. We've already got plans to take your woman out tomorrow night. How do you feel about male strip clubs?" Cruz asked.

"She's not going to a strip club," Butch said.

"You're not going to a strip club tonight?" Cheryl asked, brow raised.

"Hell, no," Butch said. "We better fucking not be."

"Stop being such a pussy. We're not going to a strip club. We're going to have a drink, celebrate the birth of a new life, and he'll be home, promise."

"Good, good. Bring him home to me in one piece." She kissed Butch's lips. "Have fun and think of me."

"Always." As selfish as it sounded even in his head, he was counting down the days until he could make love to her. He'd already circled the day on the calendar, after Christmas, but it was still there. That day, Ned would be babysitting, and he was going to spend the entire day screwing his wife. Simple as that.

Kissing his woman one final time, he followed his boys out of the house, closing the door behind him.

"You know you didn't need to do this, right?" Butch asked.

"We know it, but come on, you had a baby. Why not celebrate it?" Cruz asked.

"My wife did all the work."

"You helped. You actually got all busy and put that baby right where it needed to be," Cruz started to pump his hips doing some weird grinding action and making sounds along with it.

"He does that and wonders why no women want to fuck him," Mistletoe said.

"Women want to fuck me. They line up to get a bit of the Cruz action."

"I think I threw up in my mouth," Javier said. "Cruz action?"

"Yeah, no woman is ever the same when they've sucked some Cruz dick."

"You know, no woman is ever safe when they've been near you. They're always trying to hide, that's for sure," Butch said, slapping Cruz on the back, and climbing into the passenger side in the front of the car. Javier took the wheel while Mistletoe and Cruz sat in the back.

"You want me to show you just how good my dick can be. I can show you right here and right now."

"Dude, no one wants or needs to see your dick. Keep that shit to yourself. Man, why do I have to sit with him?" Mistletoe asked, leaning forward so that he was holding onto Javier's chair.

"Because, I'm driving and Butch is partying

tonight. Sit the fuck back," Javier said.

As Mistletoe sat back, Cruz pretended to try to make out with him.

Butch laughed.

"So, you thought about any of what we've been talking about?" Javier asked.

"I have, and I'm going to talk to Lash."

"You leaving The Skulls?"

"No, I'm not." He'd already spoken to Cheryl about that.

The Skulls were his family. He didn't want to leave that part of his life behind. What he wanted was the opportunity to expand.

Still, it was something he was going to bring forward. If Lash didn't accept, then he'd have to consider his options.

Javier pulled up into a parking lot. Climbing out, Butch took a deep breath of the warm, humid air.

He followed his friends as they headed into a bar, and started to work their way down the strip.

He had no interest in strippers or gambling.

Knocking back a couple of beers and shots, he started to get a buzz. He watched as Cruz scared a couple of women away and laughed at his attempt to even try to get them to suck his dick.

By eleven, he was feeling the effects of the alcohol, and they'd settled into a nightclub. He ordered the round for his friends and noticed out of the corner of his eye Javier tensing up.

"What is it?" Butch asked.

"That guy," Javier said. "The one that grabbed the girl, he's the one that beat the shit out of Punk."

Fortunately, he wasn't drunk enough to not see.

Butch stared at the guy.

One of the girls was trying to get free, but

whoever this piece of shit was didn't seem to care.

"You sure?"

"Fucking positive. Someone got the fight on camera. They even sent it to Punk, and I got it." Cruz held up his phone, playing the video of Punk getting his ass kicked.

Butch wasn't happy. Punk was just a kid.

"Let's go and see what he's got to say." Leaving the bar, Butch made his way over.

"Get off me," the girl said, trying to get away.

"No can do, babe. You're coming with me tonight, and you won't be complaining when I slide my dick all the way home."

"Let her go. She doesn't want you," Butch said.

He stared at the man who'd put Punk in the hospital.

Ned had been fucked off since Punk's incident. His reputation was on the line, and of course, men thought they could now take on any of Ned's fighters.

Butch would never understand why one bad fighter would tarnish them all, and yet that was exactly what was happening.

In the past few days, he'd seen it.

"Who the fuck do you think you are?" the guy said.

"Come on, Rhodes, we got to go," another guy with him said.

Butch stared at the man. Rhodes was a well-known name, especially in the ring. His reputation for cheating preceded him. Ned wouldn't have any of his fighters go against Rhodes, mainly because he'd been known to cheat and grab a weapon from one of his guys.

If Rhodes started to lose, then he'd fight dirty.

"Look, man, fuck off," Rhodes said.

"You and I have got some unfinished business,"

CHRISTMAS COMES BUTCH ONCE A YEAR

Butch said.

He felt the anger at seeing Punk beaten up, bloody, and bruised. This man's reputation, Butch had seen him many years ago in the ring, when he first came to Vegas. Ned had shown him the ropes, taught him everything he knew, and in a way, Butch became the son he never had. This business, the fighters, would never go to Eva, nor would it go to Tiny. It would come to him. He knew the work. This was his life, and this was what he wanted to bring to The Skulls.

"I don't know you."

"I know you. You think you can go around, taking on Ned Walker's fighters? I tell you, you ain't seen nothing yet."

Rhodes laughed. "You want to take me on? You think you're ready for that. Come on then, asshole, let's do this if you think you've got what it takes."

Butch was tempted to land the first blow right then. Instead, he moved out of the way for Rhodes to lead outside.

"What the hell are you going to do, man?" Javier asked.

"Keep the other men back."

"You think they're going to jump you?" Cruz asked.

"I don't doubt it. They're going to try and take me out and I won't let them. I got no interest in them. I want Rhodes. People need to learn that when you take on a fighter, you take on all of us."

"You're starting to sound like a Skull there."

"What can I say, we're all family. You don't want to stand by your friends and your fellow fighters, get the fuck out. Ned Walker doesn't compete his best fighters against each other. That's not going to happen on my watch. Not now, not ever. This piece of shit needs to be taught a lesson, and I'm going to be the one to do it."

Heading outside, he saw Rhodes was ready.

Keeping his jacket on, Butch watched as Rhodes cracked his knuckles and stretched his neck. He also kept on eye on the man's friends.

Whatever was going to go down, he was going to make sure it was a fair fight. He trusted the men at his back.

"This is for Punk," Butch said.

Stepping up to the man, he dodged the first hit and the second. Swinging out, he clocked him under the chin, and then downward, hitting both sides of the man's face. Satisfaction filled him at seeing the shock on Rhodes's face.

Rhodes had never faced a real competitor before, and now he had.

****

"You know, you didn't have to sit with me. I can take care of myself," Cheryl said. She picked up the box of Christmas decorations and placed them on the dining room table.

Ned looked like the perfect grandpa as he held Jade in his arms. He was feeding her from one of the bottles she'd already pumped that morning.

She liked to pump daily as otherwise her breasts felt so sensitive.

"I know, but I also don't mind helping out. Besides, the partying scene is not my thing anymore."

Thinking about Ned partying and dancing made her giggle.

"You be careful, girl," he said.

"Were you ever a rave kind of guy who partied?"

"I did a lot when I was younger. I had my fair share of nights out with the guys. Partying, living it up."

"What happened?"

"One day I was staring at my little girl. I'd scrubbed blood from my hands so I didn't touch her with it, and I knew I had to give it up. It was time to grow up. Eva woke me up to a lot of shit I hadn't even realized I was going through. It just goes to show you how much your kids change you."

"You don't talk a lot about that time," she said.

"There's no point. You get to be my age and you realize that what little time you've spent on this world, could have been spent doing a lot of other things. I didn't want this life for my girl. She ran from me and then met Tiny, and I had hoped she'd find someone different. Someone better than me, but that hasn't happened."

"Tiny's a good man," Cheryl said.

"Nah, he won't ever be good enough for my girl."

"Really? I thought you and Tiny got along."

"We get along because we have to. We've got an agreement that we won't argue. I won't kill him, and he won't come after me. So long as Eva's alive, he's safe."

"I don't believe you. I've seen the two of you together."

"Good acting. I know he makes my girl happy, and that is all I need from him right now."

She nodded, pulling out a worn-looking wreath.

"You can't put that up. I feel sad and completely out of the Christmas spirit just looking at it. I'll make a list of everything we need to make this house looking great."

"You love Christmas?"

"Best time of the year."

"You do surprise me."

"Why would that surprise you?" Ned asked.

"I don't know. I figured you were grumpy."

"Because I'm old?"

She shrugged.

"I'm not grumpy. I love Christmas. When Eva was young, I even attempted to learn to bake, and that was a disaster, I tell you. Nothing worse than mistaking salt and sugar. Worst thing I ever did. Eva begged me not to cook or bake a thing again."

There was a smile on his lips, and she knew it was because he was having great memories.

"You sound awesome."

"I did my best, and I've come to the conclusion that it is all we can do. Our best."

Jade finished her bottle, and Cheryl watched as he placed her against his shoulder and started to rub her back.

"Did you wish you had more kids?"

"Sometimes. Like now. Holding her, it does bring back some of the best memories of my life. Eva was a blessing to me. It's why I try to be involved as much with my grandkids as possible. It doesn't help that we're so far apart."

"I'm pleased that you're here though, and I appreciate you."

"I'll be here. I think you and Butch are good people."

She nodded and finished pulling out some twinkling lights and decorations. Michael had packed this box the previous year, and he'd just dumped everything inside.

"We've got more than enough to get us started, so I think we can just dive in and hope for the best."

Jade let out a little burp.

"Right, let's settle her in and I'll help you."

Ned put Jade down on her play mat, and Cheryl smiled as she watched her daughter. She was close by so they could attend to her if needed.

Working together, they unraveled the Christmas

lights, and Ned started to pin up some of the decorations that she loved to have hanging from the ceiling.

Once that was all done, she put Jade to bed, and took a shower. She changed into a pair of pajamas and headed downstairs to find Ned sitting on the sofa, flicking through the channels.

"She go down okay?"

"Of course. She's a good girl."

Settling on the other end of the sofa, she held a pillow and watched as Ned went up and down the channels. He'd stop for a few seconds before he got bored.

She tried not to get into anything.

"Can I ask you something?" she asked.

"Anything."

"Is it possible for Butch to start a charter here of The Skulls?" She saw Ned had paused. "Have I just broken some MC club rule or something?"

"No, not at all. I'm surprised Lash hasn't come forward sooner, to be honest. Clubs expand into new territories, and no one is in Vegas. I always expected a club to move in, but between the mafia and cartels, I think it scared people away. They don't have turf here. It could be dangerous though, him starting up."

"You don't seem surprised about me asking this."

"I think Butch has a certain quality about him. I've seen the way he's been with the fighters, and he's got what it takes to lead. I figure he needs to prove something to himself, to Lash, to the club."

"You're not happy with the club right now?"

"Oh, I'm happy with it. I don't mind the path they're on. It's their club. I don't really have much say in it. It just makes my life a lot harder." Ned shrugged. "People move forward. They change. Butch has what it takes to be a damn good Prez, and yes, it's possible for

Butch to expand, but that will have to be Lash's choice as well."

"And if he says no?" she asked.

"If Lash says no, then Butch will either have to fight for it or walk away."

"He'd never walk away from The Skulls. They're his family. He loves them."

"I know."

"Should I do something? Should I call Lash? Alex? I don't know. I just want to help him, you know. I feel that everything I do, I end up making it worse for him."

Ned put a hand on hers. "Don't stress about it. Don't worry. Allow things to fall where they may. You can't change what is going to happen. Have a little faith."

Just then the door opened, and in spilled Javier, Mistletoe, Cruz, and Butch.

The first thing she noticed was Butch's bloodied hands. Getting to her feet, she rushed toward her husband.

She expected to find him intoxicated, but he was actually in a really chipper mood.

"I did the deed," Butch said. "The fucker that took on Punk. I handled him."

"You did?" Ned got to his feet.

"It was Rhodes."

"I hate that cheating fucker," Ned said.

"What the hell is he talking about?" Cheryl asked. She let out a gasp as Butch wrapped his arm around her neck and pulled her back.

"Fighter stuff, baby. Nothing you need to worry about."

"Shh, Jade's asleep." Their baby started to cry.

"I'll go," Ned said. "It looks like you need to play nurse."

"It was so fucking cool. You should have seen him. Pow-pow, Rhodes went down, and then his friends were trying to drag him up. He went for his knife," Cruz said, showing with his fists what happened.

"If it was that easy, why are his knuckles bloody?"

"It took a few more hits, and then his buddies decided to have a turn," Butch said.

Grabbing his hand, she walked him into the kitchen. "Come on, before they become infected and I hear you moaning like a girl."

"I missed you tonight, babe."

"Did you have a good night?" she asked.

"It could have been better."

"It could have?"

"Yes, I could have been with you. Damn, I can't wait until January because I'm going to fuck you so that you'll forget every single other man in this world."

She grabbed the first aid kit. "You are drunk."

"Only on love. Lots of love."

She attended his cuts and found herself falling for him all over again. That was what she loved about Butch. He was a man of many layers, and she found herself in love with every single part of him.

****

Back at Fort Wills

"You know, you've been staring at your cell phone for an hour," Angel said, crawling on the bed and wrapping her arms around Lash's neck.

"Did you hear the news?"

"What news?"

"Cheryl had a baby. A healthy girl."

"We need to send flowers and something to welcome the new baby. Maybe we can throw a baby shower. I can do that."

"Have the whole clubhouse in pink again?" Lash asked.

She smiled and kissed his cheek. "You loved it being in pink."

He stroked her arms, and she saw he was still deep in thought.

"Okay, now you know you're going to have to tell me what is going on in that head of yours. You look way too deep in thought, and I know you've been losing sleep because of it."

He rubbed at his temples, and she moved to sit beside him on the bed. Taking his hand, she locked their fingers together, and like so many times before, stayed silent.

Lash didn't like to tell her everything that went on in the club. She knew being the Prez troubled him daily. He worried about all the decisions he made, past and present. If something really bothered him, he'd either talk to her or go to Tiny.

She was surprised he hadn't gone to Tiny, so she had to wonder if the reason had to do with Tiny. She tried to think of anything that could give a clue as to what he was thinking about.

"It's Butch."

"Oh," she said. She wouldn't have figured that out. "Because of the baby?"

"No. It was one of the last decisions Tiny made."

"You voted him out, right?" she asked. "For him to go to Vegas, to help out Ned?"

"It was. It was part of his punishment for that shit that went down with the Savage Brothers."

"And now?"

"I don't know what to do. He's a piece of the club that I've always felt was unfinished."

"Are you wanting to kick him out?" she asked,

confused.

"No. I don't want to kick him out. I've got some ideas, but I don't … it has been so long since I last saw him, I don't know what to do."

"I know Alex and Michael saw them. Why not talk to Alex?"

"I need to go to Vegas, but I think I need to talk to the club. I've got an idea I've been playing with, and I want to see what the other guys think about it first."

"You can't tell me?" she asked.

He cupped her cheek. "I can, but then I'd have to bend you over this bed and fuck you."

"Oh, I like the sound of that. Tell me."

Lash ran his thumb across her bottom lip. "You're perfection."

"I'm yours."

Chapter Eight

"They're pretty," Cheryl said.

Butch carried the large bouquet of flowers to the dining room table. Cheryl came out of the kitchen, wiping her hands as she looked at them.

"Who are they from?" she asked.

He pulled out the card and opened it up. "Congratulations on the new arrival. I can't wait to meet her. Thinking of you. Love, Lash, Angel, and The Skulls."

She placed a hand on his shoulder. "You okay?"

"Yeah, I'm good."

He stared down at the card though. Ever since he'd dealt with Punk's problem, he'd been focusing on training the fighter Ned picked out for the special Christmas fight. The card, The Skulls, it reminded him of what he had to do.

It wasn't what he had to do, but what he needed to do.

"I need to make a couple of calls, babe. You okay here?" he asked.

"Of course. I'm more than fine here."

He took her hand, kissed her inner wrist, and left the house. He walked out to the back yard and pulled out his cell phone.

He dialed Lash's number and waited for him to pick up.

"I take it your wife got my flowers."

"If I didn't know how besotted you were with your woman, I'd have assumed you wanted mine."

Lash laughed. "Not a chance. So, not that it's not great to hear from you, but why are you calling?"

Butch paused. "You and I need to talk," he said.

"Yeah, we really do. Look, there's something I

want to ask of you, but I don't want to do it over the phone. I'm heading down there in three days. You think you can put me up and we'll talk?"

"You're leaving Angel alone?"

"This is club business, and I'm not bringing her there."

"Sure, we'll put you up."

"Okay. It was good speaking to you, brother."

Lash ended the call, and Butch pocketed his cell phone.

He didn't know why Lash wanted to talk to him.

As he entered his home, the scent of cinnamon cookies overtook his senses.

"You've been baking again?" he asked, wrapping his arms around her.

"I did put them in the oven before you even answered the door," she said. "They should be ready for you now."

She pushed out of his arms and went to the oven. He watched her bend over, admiring the curves of her ass.

"How is the fight coming?" she asked.

"How do you know about that?"

"I think Ned trusts me. He talks about everything."

Butch had noticed that Ned had a loose mouth when it suited him, and when it didn't, there was never getting anything out of him.

She pulled the tray of cookies from the oven, placing them on the counter. She put two on the cooling rack, and he stole one, biting into the hot cookie.

They were his favorite, and she knew it.

Closing his eyes, he released a moan. "These are the best."

"Good. I know you love them."

"Lash is coming down," he said.

Her eyes went wide. "He is? Do you know what for?"

Butch shrugged. "He said he was talking to the club about something. It's club business."

"Do you want me to stay somewhere else?"

"Not a chance." He finished the last bite of cookie. "This is our home. He wants to talk business, we'll do it at the gym. Simple as that."

"Should I be worried?" she asked.

"There's nothing to be worried about." He pulled her into his arms and pressed his lips against hers. "What will be, will be."

She rested her head against his chest, and he breathed in her scent.

Part of him was worried.

For some time now, he'd felt this sense of unease, like he had to make a choice.

A choice that would change his and his family's life forever.

The sound of the doorbell ringing had him kissing her head. "I'll get that."

"How did you like the cookies?" she asked.

"They're the best ones ever. Thank you, baby."

He walked toward the front door, and he was shocked to see Ned, Javier, Mistletoe, Cruz, and Punk at his front door.

"Merry Christmas," they all said.

"What the hell are you guys doing?" he asked.

"Well, we didn't get a chance to take Cheryl out, so we thought we'd bring a party here," Javier said.

"We've got sleeping bags," Cruz said, holding up his little bundle.

"Oh, so you think of coming to my house and even inviting yourself in for the night?"

"Hell, yeah," Javier said. "Just be thankful he didn't bring a woman with him. He saw a couple he wanted to bring back."

"What's this?" Cheryl asked, coming to the door.

"They want to celebrate Jade's birth at our house where we have to clean everything up."

She rolled her eyes. "Why not? You're only going to eat all those cookies by yourself and then complain about needing to go to the gym."

"I work at the gym every single day," he said.

"Exactly, you should work harder." She winked at him.

"Actually, this isn't just a celebration for Jade's birth," Ned said. "Cheryl, honey, you didn't get a baby shower."

"She doesn't know any chicks to do one for her," Mistletoe said.

"So, we banded together and decided to be the chicks for you," Punk said.

"This is a combined baby shower and congratulations. We have gifts and goodies, and I even have some punch that has no alcohol in it," Cruz said. "Butch told us you were breastfeeding."

"Stay away from that horny bastard. He gets off on everything," Butch warned.

He watched his friends enter his home, and they all walked into the living room. He closed the door and leaned against the sitting room doorway, observing his friends.

Vegas, when he'd first arrived with Cheryl and Michael, had seemed like a bad place. They were far from the small town that he was accustomed to. Their time had been stressful, and he recalled the nights he heard Cheryl cry.

He'd felt overwhelming guilt, but now, after all

these years, they were a family. He knew she missed Michael. Letting him go had been one of the hardest decisions they'd ever made.

Alex would always visit him, and sometimes the tensions would run way too high. He didn't know how to stop it. They all had a history, and it made it hard for Michael.

He watched as she opened the gifts his friends had bought for her. One of them was indeed a breast pump from Cruz.

"Wow, Cruz, this is so thoughtful," she said.

"Yeah, I heard about how uncomfortable it is for a woman if your kid's not hungry. I didn't know if your man here would be willing to suck it all out for you."

Cheryl's cheeks were bright red. "I never thought of that."

"You have to, you know. It's right up there as something that needs to be dealt with. You don't want to be storing sour milk, and you know if you're ever desperate, I will sacrifice my respect and help you."

Butch hit him around the back of the head. "Don't even think of putting your lips anywhere near my woman."

"Hey, I was offering to help her. You don't have to go around beating me." Cruz rubbed the back of his head.

"He's a weird one. Don't worry about it," Butch said.

Cheryl was still laughing as she unwrapped the final present, which was a robe and pajamas for her. The breast pump, the stroller, along with baby bottles, pacifiers, and clothes—it was all so incredibly sweet.

"Thank you," she said. She gave each man a hug and a kiss on the cheek.

Finally, she came to him. "And thank you."

"What did I do?"

"You made all of this possible, and I love you for it. You're a good man, Butch. I hope Lash and the others see that."

He wrapped his arms around her waist. "I hope he sees it as well."

"Come on, you two, stop smooching. Let's get this tree up," Cruz said, getting to his feet and standing in front of the naked fir tree.

"How old are you?" Butch asked.

"Old enough to still love Christmas. It's that time of the year for everyone and not just kids."

"Don't even get me started, Butch. When we're at the mall, he'll sit on Santa's lap," Javier said.

"And demand his picture be taken with him," Mistletoe said.

"Seriously?" Butch looked toward Cruz.

"There are some things in life that need adulting. In other aspects, people can kiss my hairy fucking ass."

He grabbed the ornaments he'd put near the stairs and brought them in.

Cruz was the first one there, and Butch stood back as his friends began to put the decorations on the tree.

It felt surreal.

He hadn't experienced this since he'd last been in Fort Wills, which right now felt like a lifetime ago.

Cheryl moved toward him, placing a hand beneath around his back. "You okay?"

"Yeah, I'm just … I'm feeling it, you know."

"What are you feeling?" she asked.

"Family. It's right here."

"I know." She rested her head against his chest.

Kissing her brow, he watched the guys assemble his tree. It looked a mess, but he'd fix it when they were gone.

For now, it was more than okay to have some fun.

****

Three days later

"You're seriously cleaning the gym?" Ned asked.

Cheryl held the duster in her hand. Jade was in his office, sleeping away. The guys were all fighting and doing their training. She knew the special Christmas fight was just a few days away.

Still, her mind was on her man, who'd gone to get Lash from the airport. She felt so incredibly stressed.

Butch had opened up to her and admitted how much this meant to him.

He wanted to expand The Skulls. The last thing he wanted to do was to create his own club, but he knew his options were limited.

Going back home wasn't an option. He couldn't do it. Too much time had passed.

His love and loyalty were still there, but he just couldn't bring himself to go back.

There had to be a point to move forward.

"It's dirty," she said.

"It's a gym."

"And it needs cleaning."

Ned closed the book he was writing in, removed his glasses, and stared at her. "What's going on?"

"Nothing."

"You have that worried look. Now, Jade is down, so she's out for a few hours. What's up?"

She nibbled her lip. "Butch."

"What about it?"

"You know he's gone to meet Lash, right?"

"I'm aware, and I also know what he's hoping to discuss. Is this bothering you?"

"I just, I don't know what to do. I want to be

there for him, and I'm not. I'm right here. Ugh, this sucks."

"Honey, you're not going to be able to do anything about what they're discussing. This is between Butch and Lash. Not you."

"I know, but he's my old man."

Ned chuckled. "It's good to be worried. It'll keep you alive, but you have to give your man space to make these negotiations."

"Do you think Lash will agree?" Cheryl asked.

Ned put his glasses back on, and she saw him staring across the room. "Tiny would have disagreed."

"He would?"

"Yep."

"How do you know that?"

"I know Tiny. The Skulls, other than their Nomad chapter, was all about staying in Fort Wills. It's the one part of his ruling as Prez I always found irritating."

"So, do you think Lash is the same?"

Ned tapped his fingers on the board. "No. It's not. Lash has made a lot of decisions and major changes. For the most part, I've not seen them coming, and no, before you even ask, I've not liked them. To be fair, he's done what the club has needed at the time, and I can't fault the kid for that. He's got the role exactly right for what he needs to do."

"But?"

"But again, this is all down to Lash, really. Opening a new clubhouse, expanding, that is a big deal."

"I know it is, but I know Butch can do it."

"You sound like a little girl begging Santa. Cheryl, you're just going to have to wait and see what happens."

"Waiting sucks." She dropped down onto his sofa, folding her arms and sticking out her lip.

"You're adorable when you have a temper tantrum. Don't ever complain to me when Jade does it."

She couldn't help it. She stuck out her tongue and glanced at the clock. Ned's laughter echoed around the room, and her heart raced. She hoped Butch knew what he was doing.

****

"It has been too long," Lash said.

Butch slapped Lash on the back as they hugged. "The Prez look is suiting you."

"It is? I'm sure I've got a grey hair. Look at this." Lash pointed out a tuft of hair that looked its usual color. "The club is making me old before my time. I'm not going to last much longer. Congratulations on the kid, man."

"Thanks. Want to see her picture?" Butch got his cell phone out and pulled up the pictures of his daughter. There was one of Michael and Jade as well.

"She's so pretty," Lash said. "You're going to have to be ready to fucking kill any little shit that comes within sniffing distance of her."

"That I will." Butch laughed.

"It's good to see Michael looking happy."

"He doing good?"

"Yeah, he is."

"We're going to invite Michael, Alex, Sunshine, and their kids here for Christmas."

"It sounds very much like a blended family."

"It is." They made their way out of the airport toward the waiting car.

Taking Lash's bags, he threw them into the trunk and climbed behind the wheel. Lash was already on his cell phone, typing away.

"Just letting my woman know I'm safe and sound."

"She doesn't trust you with me?"

"She does. I know she worries though."

"I get that. I'll take us to Ned's."

"You know what, take us to a bar."

"You want to go to a bar?"

"Hell, yeah. We need to talk, and Ned and I don't always see eye to eye."

"You want a titty club?" Butch asked.

"No. I've got a woman waiting for me at home."

"You don't cheat on Angel?"

"You really want to ask me that?" Lash asked.

"Just making conversation."

"I could ask that about you and Cheryl."

"Go ahead, I've got nothing to hide. I'd never cheat on my woman."

"Angel's my world. I just want a quiet bar, Butch. We've got some things to discuss."

It was still early, but the thing about Vegas, it never slept, so he found them a quiet bar. Butch entered first and went straight to the bar, ordering them both a drink. Lash found them a quiet booth.

Taking a seat, he waited as Lash took a sip of the cheap-ass whiskey he'd bought him.

"It's nasty, but it'll do."

"Why are you here, Lash?"

"Same reason you called me up, Butch. This deal where you stay in Vegas, you and I know it's unfinished business. The Skulls is changing. I was one of the votes that decided for you to leave."

"As with every single club brother."

"It wasn't easy. There was a lot of shit going down, and you made some shitty choices."

"I know what I did."

In the world of MC, there was no place for shared loyalties. The moment the Savage Brothers MC approached him, he should have gone to Tiny. Instead, he'd kept it to himself and tried to work for both clubs, seeing as they wanted the same kind of end. It had blown up in his face, and he'd been living with the consequences ever since.

"You know I'm not going to fuck this up anymore. My loyalty to you and to the club is solid."

"I know that. The entire club knows that." Lash knocked back his whiskey. "I know in this world you either have to constantly be moving, or you're going to get run over and something or someone is going to try and take your place. I never saw how fucking dangerous it was being Prez when Tiny was in this spot. He made a lot of choices along the way that I didn't care for."

"We were living in dangerous times."

"But those times are coming to an end. You know the club is no longer running guns or drugs for Ned. We're out. Completely clean. Chaos Bleeds is doing it as well."

"I'd heard Devil had decided to pull out."

"We're all tired, Butch. We're all tired, and we need to know our family is safe." Lash stared into his glass.

The tension in the air seemed to rise.

"Butch, before I continue any further, I need to know if you're wanting to come back to Fort Wills. If you're wanting to take your spot at the table," Lash said.

Butch stared at him. This had been a question he'd been dreading.

"I don't want you to bullshit me. Just answer my question."

"When I first moved out of here, I'd have given anything and everything to be back in Fort Wills." He stared around the bar. "I don't know what it is, but something in Vegas changes you."

"It's Ned, he rubs off on you."

"I happen to like Ned."

"We don't want Ned unprotected. He's pissed at me and the clubs right now, but we know he's an ally. We care about him."

"That man is going to outlive us all," Butch said.

"Answer the question," Lash said.

"No, I don't want a spot at the table. Fort Wills is not my home anymore. Too much time has passed." He thought about Javier, Mistletoe, Cruz, Punk, and even Ned. Fuck, he'd somehow managed to create a family here.

"That's what I figured." Lash reached into the bag that he'd brought with him out of the car. "We took a vote. We've got the Nomad chapter, and we need someone here. Someone willing to keep an eye on Ned, to take this patch of land before another club claims it." Lash pulled out a leather cut. "And I was hoping you'd be the one willing to take on the role of Prez. It means you'll still have to deal with me. You're still a Skull, only you're the Vegas Chapter."

And that was exactly what it said on the jacket, "The Skulls, Vegas Chapter."

Butch held the jacket and ran his thumb across the patch that titled him Prez.

"You're serious."

"As a fucking heart attack. It was a unanimous vote, Butch. Some of the guys will head out here, you know, for parties and shit, and we'll help you be part of the initiations for the club. You need to make sure they're fucking good."

"I will. I've got three candidates already," he said, thinking about Cruz, Javier, and Mistletoe.

"Then I'll meet them. You're going to be responsible for the setup. You need a clubhouse, a base, something to call your own." Lash reached into his bag and handed over an envelope. "Here's a hundred grand to get you started. When you have a place, call me, and I'll wire you the other cash."

"Why are you doing this?" Butch asked.

"It's good for the club. You and I both know that you were never meant to be a brother. It's in your blood to lead, and I'm giving you that option. Take it or leave it."

He took the money and shook Lash's hand.

He wasn't going to fucking cry.

"Welcome to the fold, brother."

They left the bar, and Butch removed his leather Skulls cut, handing it to Lash, who rolled it up and placed it in the bag.

Pulling on his new leather cut, it felt right. The leather wasn't worn in yet, but with time, he'd have it ready.

"It looks damn good."

Climbing into the car, he took Lash toward the gym where he knew Cheryl and the guys would be waiting. He'd called them as he arrived at the airport and told them to get down to the gym.

"Do you like being Prez?" Butch asked.

"It's okay. I'm not going to lie, it's fucking tough. I worry about every fucking choice I make. The one with Kelsey's ex being the fucking biggest one I've made."

Kelsey's ex, Michael Granito, worked for a special force within the Fed office. The Skulls acted as witness protection for victims. They helped to protect while the law did the work to put them behind bars.

When they arrived at the gym, it looked empty.

Butch locked the car.

"You know you're going to have to get a bike,

right? We're still a fucking MC," Lash said.

"I'll deal with that."

"Why aren't you riding a bike?" Lash asked.

"It kept getting stolen."

Lash burst out laughing. "Seriously?"

"It's not fucking funny."

"It is to me. It's so funny. Holy shit, what the fuck have I just done? You can't even keep a bike."

"You're not taking this shit back."

"I've no intention of doing that, but come on, man, that is fucking priceless. I'm making you Prez of a brand-new fucking chapter, and you can't even keep a bike from being stolen. Wow, this is going to be so funny."

Butch didn't appreciate his sense of humor.

Entering the gym, he saw Cheryl was waiting for him. She held Jade in her arms, and the moment she saw him, she stood.

Javier, Mistletoe, and Cruz were all there waiting.

"Well, well, well, old man Ned, you're still alive and kicking," Lash said.

Ned came out of his office.

"Fuck me, you're getting older every single time I see you."

They shook hands, and Ned pulled Lash in against him, slapping him on the back.

"Are you okay?" Cheryl asked.

Her gaze went to his leather cut, and her eyes went wide. "Seriously?" She gasped and covered her mouth with her hand.

"Yes, seriously."

She touched the cut right where it declared him as Prez.

"Say hello to the brand-new Prez of The Skulls, Vegas Chapter." Lash pointed at him. "It had to happen eventually."

"You got Tiny to agree to this?" Ned asked.

"It was a unanimous vote. We all know how important it is in this world to keep on moving forward. There's our guy." Lash looked toward the three men. "I take it these are the guys you want?"

"Yes."

"They're going to have to go through some testing," Lash said. "You need to make sure they're loyal."

"We are fucking loyal," Cruz said. "We've got Butch's back."

"It's not just about Butch. It's about having the name, the entire club at your back."

"They do," Butch said. "As soon as we have a base, you can come and check it out."

"We will," Lash said.

Butch saw the warning in Lash's eyes.

His friends may be his friends, but that didn't mean they had what it took to be a Skull. Butch knew without a doubt they'd pass their tests.

Holding Cheryl to his side, he smiled down at her.

This was what he wanted, and he was going to make damn sure that it worked.

Chapter Nine

Lash stayed for two days before returning back to Fort Wills. It was kind of surreal to have him stay at their house, but Cheryl loved it, especially hearing about everything that was going on in The Skulls. What she didn't like was hearing about Darcy. That did break her heart.

She hoped to hear more soon, but as they were in Vegas, she doubted they would be the first ones to be called of any new developments.

As for Christmas, Alex, Sunshine, and their kids came to visit. Michael as well, and for the first time in all of their lives together, they had a Christmas together as a blended family, together as one big family.

Sunshine helped her with the Christmas dinner while Butch, Alex, and Michael all planned the coming year.

They didn't stay for the New Year, but it gave her hope.

Of course, Butch was hunting for a new place to call his own. They wanted one close to the gym, and Ned was also there, helping them pick out a place. Butch had turned down three possible spots for the clubhouse. He didn't want to be so far away that it would leave them easy pickings, but he also wanted to look to possibly expand.

She went with him on every single trip, taking the baby with her. Ned was always on hand to help out when needed with the clubhouse or with babysitting, or Javier did.

This new development in their lives had taken over completely.

Finally, by the end of January, they pulled up to the place that was twenty minutes' walk from the gym. It was an old junkyard. The old cars and used parts were all gone, and the building looked like it needed some serious repair. Climbing out of the car, she looked up at the used building.

Butch had looked really excited about this place, but she just saw one big hazard.

"What do you think?" he asked.

"You're going to need to knock it all down and start again."

"Have some vision, Cheryl."

"I am."

"You go on in and show her. I'll stay with Jade," Ned said.

She looked back at Ned, wishing she had the excuse not to follow Butch into the old, crumbling building.

"Have a little faith in your old man."

"I've got a lot of faith, Butch. What I'm worried about is if you've lost your damn mind."

He grabbed her hand and pulled her into the building. It was indeed crumbling, and it looked like a piece of shit.

She stood in the center of the building and held her hands to her side. She didn't want to touch anything. There seemed to be way too many spiders and other things.

"Look, these are good walls. It's not falling down," Butch said, pressing his hand against the wall. "I've spoken to a building contractor. He knows his shit. He can get this place set up, and he believes we can have it ready by the end of the year."

"It's January."

"There's a lot of work to do. What do you think?"

She tried not to cringe.

Butch wrapped his arms around her. "I know you

don't see it now, but this place is going to be something. Do you trust me?"

"You know I do."

"Then give me that smile I love and I know I can handle everything."

She gave him that smile.

"That's what I needed." He pulled her in close, and his lips brushed across hers. "This is it, Cheryl. I can feel it."

"I hope you don't expect me to deal with the spiders."

"Don't worry about it. I'll set Cruz on them. They'll handle everything." He kissed her neck. "I've talked to Ned."

She gasped as he sucked on her pulse. "You have."

"You think I've forgotten my promise to you?"

"I don't know."

"I've not forgotten, and tonight, you're all mine. Ned is going to take Jade for us."

"You're sure he doesn't mind?"

"He doesn't mind. With Jade out of the house that means you're going to be able to scream as I lick your pussy, fucking you so hard you can't even think straight, and then I'm going to take your ass."

She moaned as he gripped her ass, drawing her close. "I thought you didn't want to anymore."

"The club is important, finding a base for us all is important, but you are even more so." He kissed her again. "Now, how about we head out? Drop Ned off at his place, and I take you home."

"That sounds … wonderful."

Butch took her hand, and they made their way outside. Ned was waiting in the car.

"What do you think?" Ned asked.

"It looks good."

"We're dropping you and Jade off, Ned. Like you promised."

"What did I promise?" Ned asked.

"To take care of Jade so we can have some us time," Butch said.

"I don't think I agreed to that."

"Butch, you can't just do that," Cheryl said, her cheeks heating with every passing second.

"I have dropped my plans to help this bastard every step of the way. You want to help me save my marriage, you'll take care of our daughter for me."

She covered her face with her hands, in complete shock as Butch did indeed drop Ned and Jade off. He had a bag already prepared, one she didn't even realize he'd done.

Within an hour, they were alone, in their home, and before he'd even shut the door completely, he had her pinned against the wall. He shoved the door, and it closed.

"I cannot wait another minute. I've been waiting too long for this." With Butch's growl echoing in the air, he began to tear at her clothes.

Cheryl wasn't fighting or arguing. She needed him just as much as he needed her.

Her body was on fire, and it was all for him.

Tearing at his clothes, she cried out his name as he cupped her pussy. Kicking their clothes onto the floor, she wrapped her arms around his neck as he lifted her up. His cock poised at her entrance, she felt him, inch by inch, sinking deep inside her, going to the hilt, shocking her at the depth, as with the final inches, he slammed in hard.

"Oh, fuck," she said.

"So fucking tight. I've missed this. I've missed

your pussy. I've missed being inside you. It has been sheer torture, baby. You have no idea."

"Shut up. Fuck me, please, Butch."

He pulled out of her only to slam all the way to the hilt. She scored her nails down his back, holding him close as he repeatedly fucked her, over and over, driving deep within her until she couldn't see straight.

"You feel so fucking good. Never again, babe. I'm not waiting this long to be inside you. I've missed you so damn much. You have the best fucking pussy in the world."

She'd been craving his touch and feeling his dick deep inside her.

He moved her down to the floor, and, wrapping her legs around his waist, she arched up, making him go deeper. She didn't want him to stop. The very idea of him not being inside her just wasn't allowed to be a thought in her head.

"I need you, please, please."

He pulled out of her, and she missed the feeling of his cock so much she whimpered. However, he grabbed her hips, pulling her up so that his mouth was on her pussy. He began to lick and suck at her clit. His tongue slid between her slit, making her moan with every passing second as he teased her body, preparing her in every single way imaginable to take him.

She was getting so close.

He pulled away from her clit to plunge inside her, fucking her repeatedly.

She screamed his name.

"You want to come, baby? You want me to fill your pussy with my dick?"

"Yes, please, yes."

He focused on her clit, sliding back and forth across her nub until she came. The orgasm exploded behind her eyes until she saw stars. She'd never experienced so much pleasure before that it took her breath away.

Within seconds, he was back inside her, driving harder and deeper within her, each stroke only adding to her need for more of his cock.

"Oh, fuck, I'm not going to last."

He pounded inside her, going to the hilt, and she loved every second of it. Holding onto him, she felt his cock pulse as he spilled his cum within her, over and over again. His growl filled the room.

Afterward, he collapsed over her, and she took the weight. After so long without him because of being pregnant, it felt good to have him in her arms once again.

"I'm crushing you," he said.

"You're not. I love feeling you like this. I've missed this." She saw the happiness in his eyes. "Were you worried?"

"About the baby?"

"That and also about what Lash would do and say."

"I was. I didn't want to argue with him."

"You're a good man, Butch. I think over the years you've forgotten that."

"I've done bad things, and I'll continue to do bad things."

She didn't have a response to that, so she leaned up and kissed him. "I'll be by your side, regardless."

****

The club was coming along. Most of the internal work had been completed within three months, and his daughter was growing up. Butch's relationship with Cheryl continued to flourish. The problems they'd faced while she'd been pregnant were now nonexistent.

Everything was falling into place for once in his

life. He didn't want to fuck it up or jinx it.

Reeving his bike, he took off down the street, remembering the way to Punk's house. He'd made a full recovery and had yet to be seen at the gym to train. Ned had told him the kid had pulled his name off the schedule and out of the fighting ring.

It was always a fighter's choice when it came to it. None of them forced men to fight. To enter a ring, they had to be prepared for everything and anything.

If your head wasn't in the game, bad shit happened.

Simple as that.

He'd seen Ned change the lineup a few times because he didn't think fighters were ready to take on the tough shit.

Parking up outside of Punk's house, Butch turned off his ignition. Climbing off the bike, he walked up the small porch and knocked on the window.

He waited.

Staring up at the sky, he saw no stars were shining tonight. There was a time he'd spend a lot of time staring at the stars, wondering about shit. It was something he'd taken up when he was a kid after his father was murdered before him and he was left for dead.

"Butch, what are you doing here, man?" Punk closed the door behind him.

Since the last time he saw him, Punk had lost a lot of weight, and he didn't look healthy.

"Your mom inside?"

"Yeah, she's having a bad day. Whatever shit you've got to say, say it. I need to head back inside."

"This is for you," Butch said, pulling out the brown envelope and handing it to him.

"What is this?" Punk asked, taking the brown envelope.

Inside was over ten grand in cash.

"Your hospital bills have all been paid for."

"I ... what? I don't understand," Punk said. "I've not done a single thing to earn this. I can't take this."

"Rhodes is known for cheating. We saw what he did to you, and he's been repaid in kind. You're not a weak kid, Punk. The guys got together and decided who was to fight on the big night. Ned arranged it all, and we made sure the guy who went against Rhodes wasn't any pushover. This is the money raised." The fight itself didn't last all that long. Butch had attacked Rhodes, making him weak, and then one of the seasoned boys offered to finish him off. Ned made sure it was clean cut, and after that fight finished, had lined up some sporting events to keep his guests happy.

Punk looked away, and Butch saw the tears in his eyes.

"It's okay to be afraid."

"I'm not afraid."

"Rhodes had all of his men at his back. Next time you go out, you make sure you've got men you can trust. Who are willing to take a beating for you or at the very least fight back. Your friends ran away, leaving you to fend for yourself. So they're not your friends. All of the guys put this together for you. They don't expect anything back, but you've got to come back to the gym. We'll help you learn to fight, but you keep your bullshit at home, got it? Your hospital bill has been paid for. You need help, you come to me or Ned. Don't think you're on your own."

He saw the tears fall from Punk's eyes. "I heard you started a club."

"The Skulls, Vegas Chapter." He nodded.

"I want to be part of that."

"Then we'll see how you do. You're young,

Punk. You need to be willing to do a lot of shit to get in with The Skulls."

"I'll do it. Whatever it takes, I'm your guy. I can be part of it."

"Then prove it. I want you at the gym training tomorrow. I don't take no for an answer."

Turning on his heel, he walked away with a smile on his face.

Everything was good. More than good.

It was fucking fantastic.

Chapter Ten

Eight months later

Cheryl couldn't believe this day had come. For the past eight months, Butch had been working tirelessly to get this club set up, and now as each of The Skulls from Fort Wills arrived, her nerves were completely shot.

Every single week for eight months, they'd had one of The Skulls or the family staying with them, Lacey being one of the people that visited most often. She adored Lacey and Angel as well, even though she was really, really sweet.

There was a time when Cheryl found Angel too sweet and wondered if it was fake. Over time, she realized it wasn't. Angel was just a nice person, which made it even more strange that she was with Lash. That man was dangerous and really fucking scary as far as Cheryl was concerned.

"Are you excited?" Lacey asked, coming to stand beside her.

"Yeah, of course." Javier, Mistletoe, Cruz, and of course Punk were lurking around somewhere.

She'd heard all of the guys making plans for the club. Butch and Ned had also been arguing about the possible drug and gun runs.

Even though this was Butch's chapter, Lash had advised him not to go into hardcore shit.

She hated to agree with Lash, but she felt he was right, especially about this. She didn't want to have to worry about her guy getting hurt. He'd not been on any serious runs in years.

This wasn't about them getting into trouble. This was about him finding himself again.

"It looks good," Whizz said.

"You can't even see it. It's behind the curtain,"

Lacey said.

"I saw it the other day. While you were busy painting everyone's nails, I was checking on the club." Whizz wrapped his arm around her waist and pulled her close.

Cheryl watched them, and it was then she felt something twist in her gut. Even though she didn't want to go back to Fort Wills, it didn't mean she didn't miss this, seeing the couples together.

She'd been part of The Skulls for a very short time, but she'd seen the family that they were.

Even now, Lash held Angel close to him as he talked with Eva, Tiny, and Ned. She couldn't help but watch Ned to see if he let slip at any point that he didn't like Tiny.

Of course, the mask was on display, and he looked interested in whatever Tiny had to say.

She figured he was bullshitting about it all.

"Are you guys ready?" Butch asked, coming out from behind the curtain he'd put in front of the building.

She hadn't seen the finished product because she took care of Jade.

"Hey, Mom," Michael said, coming to stand beside her.

"Hey, honey." She wrapped her arms around him and hugged him close.

"Please, not now, people can see."

"I don't care if people can see. I love you." She kissed his cheek and chuckled as he wiped it away.

"You're mean."

"It's so good to have you here. How is everything at school?" she asked.

"Same as it was last night. Nothing has changed since then."

"Well, you never know, and I'm just making sure.

I don't want anything bad to happen to my baby." She ruffled his head, and he groaned. Just then, Jade chose that moment to whimper.

Reaching into the stroller, Cheryl unbuckled her and picked her up. She wasn't even a year old yet, but she was growing so strong.

"Say hello to your big brother," Cheryl said.

Michael smiled and reached out. Jade snatched his finger and tried to bite him.

She laughed as the sheet went down, and the lights were bright, showcasing the new clubhouse for The Skulls, Vegas Chapter.

There were cheers, screams, and rounds of applause.

Seeing Butch with his club again, she was so damn happy for him.

It didn't take long after the unveiling for the barbeques to be set up and a few bonfires.

Butch made the rounds, and she kept an eye on him, knowing he'd been worried.

"He made it work," Alex said, coming to stand beside her.

She turned to the man she had once crushed on and most hated. Now, she was just content.

"He did."

"Butch is a good man. He'll make one fine leader."

"I know." She sighed.

"And she is looking so beautiful and growing up so fast," Alex said.

"Yeah, she's getting her teeth, and she doesn't like that. Doesn't like pain." She kissed Jade's cheek. "Thank you."

"What are you thanking me for?"

"For Michael. For being there for him. For

helping." They hadn't sent Michael to Fort Wills just because of the baby. He'd been sent to live with his father because he'd started to fall in with the wrong crowd, and no matter what she or Butch did, he wasn't happy with them. "I don't think I've ever really thanked you for anything in my life. Not for giving me my son, or for being there."

"Cheryl, I've done a lot of bad shit myself. You've got nothing to thank me for. I only hope that we can continue as friends. I never meant to hurt you all those years ago. I was a selfish prick. I've grown a lot since then. Seen the mythical error of my ways."

This made her laugh.

"Truce?" she asked.

"Truce."

They shook hands, and finally hugged. For the first time since she met Alex, she actually felt they had gotten all of their history behind them.

It was no longer a dark cloud over them, just something in the past.

She wasn't going to hold his abandonment against him, and he wasn't going to hold her blackmail over her either.

It was done.

They were done.

They shared a son together, and they would work in his best interests.

"What is going on here?" Butch asked. "You two aren't going to kill each other, are you? I don't think that will be good for Michael."

"Nah, we're not going to do that. I'm happy for you, Butch. You've done well."

"Thanks, Alex."

She watched Alex walk away.

The family was back together for at least one

night, and she was happy about that.

"What about you? I know I can't trust him," Butch said.

She chuckled. "Maybe this time you should."

"You two are good?"

"Better than good."

"You are?"

"Yes. I think after all these years, we've finally put the past to bed."

"And you can handle that?" he asked.

"Yes, I can. It looks fantastic."

"It does."

"So, what happens now?" she asked.

"Well, all the guys are here and that's to see if Javier, Mistletoe, and Cruz can handle themselves."

"The initiation?"

"That's it. You want to go in and see where you'll be staying when you're at the club?"

"You're going to be staying here a lot?"

"Some nights but don't worry, I know who I belong to." He kissed her neck.

With Jade on her hip, she followed behind Butch as he showed her the clubhouse, the bar, and then into the main corridor of the rooms.

"It looks amazing."

Once they got to his room, he took Jade from her arms and placed her in the center of the bed.

"I know I wouldn't have been able to have done this without you," he said.

"Butch, you can do everything and anything you put your mind to." She cupped his cheek. "This is just the beginning. I don't have any doubt that this is going to be one of the fiercest clubs around." She went on her tiptoes and pressed a kiss to his lips. "I love you, forever and for always. Never forget it."

The sound of Jade gurgling interrupted them. Butch dived for his daughter as she was about to spill off the bed, and he caught her before she hit the ground.

Collapsing on the bed, he held Jade on his chest, and she settled down beside him.

"Do you want to stay here when the initiation starts?" he asked.

"I'll wait for you here." She kissed his cheek. "We can initiate this room together."

****

"Three people are not going to make a club," Nash said.

"It's a start," Butch said.

"The Skulls started out small," Tiny said. "It takes time to build a loyal club. What Butch has here is a good starting point."

Butch looked toward his old Prez and nodded at him. The respect was there between the two of them.

That's all he could ever want, especially from Tiny.

"Please, I'm worth five of you fuckers," Cruz said. "I will fuck any of you up."

"I'd be careful. To Cruz, fuck can mean two things. Bruises or your body belongs to him," Javier said.

"I'm a man of many talents, and I don't complain. I'm the best dick you've ever seen."

Butch covered his face with his hands. Even now, Cruz didn't know when to shut his mouth. Killer was the first man to enter the ring.

"Holy shit, what do they feed you in Fort Wills, magic fucking beans?" Cruz asked. "He's not real, and you're married. How do you fuck your wife without breaking her?"

The entire club was laughing. Even Killer was struggling to hold it together.

Cruz lifted his fists. "Come on then, shorty, let's get this show on the road."

"Shorty, seriously?"

"You may be big, but I'm the one with the power." Cruz raised his brows and gave a pout.

"Where did you find this guy?" Lash asked.

"He came to the gym about fifteen years ago," Ned said. "Fucker never left. I don't even think I've seen him fight."

"I have," Butch said. "Don't be fooled by his bullshit attitude. He's deadly. Watch."

The fight started, and Killer landed a couple of blows and even lifted Cruz off his feet. Even with blood pouring down his nose, and bruises covering his face, the son of a bitch didn't stop.

This was what made Cruz one hell of a buddy. He didn't stop. He would have your back and wouldn't back down. It was simple as that. Cruz never backed down from a fight, and he'd go down with his fists ready to take a beating.

When the time came, Killer left the ring, and this time, Nash was the one to fight.

Nash didn't give Cruz a chance to talk. Blow after blow, and each time Cruz got back up.

The point of the initiation was to keep taking the beating. Even when they were asked if they wanted to stop, if you said yes, you were out. No one wanted someone at their back that couldn't take a few punches.

Whizz took his turn, as did Zero, Tiny, and finally Lash.

Eventually, Cruz was still standing, admittedly, looking pretty fucking broken.

"You had enough?" Lash asked.

"Oh, please, I can take you all day. What you're giving me is fucking nothing," Cruz said. He had a bloody nose, split lip, and he looked ready to collapse in a heap.

Lash nodded.

He signaled to Steven, who brought forward the leather cut.

"I'm in?" Cruz asked.

"You're in." Lash helped him into the jacket. "Welcome to The Skulls, Vegas Chapter." Butch stepped forward, and Cruz let out a feminine moan.

"I want to thank absolutely everyone who supported me. My momma for being a crack whore who gave me up. My daddy for dumping his load and paying her in crack all those years ago." Again, more laugher filled the air. "I always wish to thank all the bitches that have sucked my dick. Without you, my balls would be like giant balloons."

Butch stepped forward. "Enough."

"I promise to never be dull. To always keep fighting and to keep fucking."

"Enough. Do I need to put you in the naughty corner?"

"Will you spank me, Daddy?" Cruz asked.

"Can I take his patch from him?"

Lash was too busy laughing with the rest of the brothers. "Not a chance."

"They love me, Butch." Cruz rested his head against his chest.

He didn't say anything and waited as both Mistletoe and Javier each took their turn to face the brothers. By the time they were done, all three had been initiated. That wasn't all. The first Prospect jacket went to Punk.

He wasn't ready to become a member. He'd been building up his skills, but he wasn't at the point of being able to take on the brothers. Butch saw his love of the club though in all the hard work he was doing.

After they all sat around the bonfire, drinking a beer, Butch leaned back, staring up at the stars.

He'd never in his wildest dreams imagined he'd be the Prez of a new chapter of The Skulls.

His father had been a Prez, as had his grandfather. He'd not thought about them for a long time.

It seemed right.

He was going full circle. There was no looking back now. He'd make this club the best it could be. Lash and the guys would be proud.

It was the start of a whole new life.

Getting to his feet, he said goodnight to the guys. Lash had already gone to spend time with Angel.

Making his way to his room, he found Cheryl curled up in the bed. Jade was already in the crib. Smiling, he padded across the room so that he didn't wake Cheryl.

He removed his clothes, settled into bed behind her, and wrapped his arms around her waist.

"Did you have a good night?" she asked, her voice filled with sleep.

"Yes."

"I love you, Butch."

"I love you too."

CHRISTMAS COMES BUTCH ONCE A YEAR

Epilogue

Ten years later

Butch threw his head back and laughed as Jade tackled him, wrapping her arms around his waist and hugging him.

"Daddy, Michael won't come and play."

"He doesn't have to."

"He's my big brother. He has to do what I say. It's the law," Jade said, stamping her foot.

He rolled his eyes and turned to look at Michael. His stepson was all grown up and had even gone to college.

Cheryl walked around the club, wearing the leather cut he loved for her to wear whenever they had big family gatherings. Tonight's celebration was about the club. For ten years the Vegas Chapter had expanded, bringing in more and more guys as they wanted to join what he'd created.

With the help from the Skulls from Fort Wills, his club had become a force to be reckoned with.

The moment he set up shop, there had been some wars.

Other MCs wanted a shot at turf. Before he'd marked this spot as his own, no one wanted it. He made sure not to give it up.

This was Skulls property, and that was exactly how it would stay.

"I'm not playing. I'm a grown-ass man," Michael said.

"I hate you." Jade folded her arms and stormed away.

"She has really turned into a brat."

"She'll head inside and make you a sorry card. All the shit for it is inside my desk."

With how much they struggled to have Jade, Butch had put his foot down, and he didn't intend to have any more kids.

His time for being a father was over.

He was there for Michael when he needed him and a father to Jade.

Cheryl walked up to him, wrapping her arms around his waist as she always did. "How are you doing, baby?"

"I'm doing good."

"Nope, still disgusting." Michael wrinkled his nose.

"It's good to have you here," Butch said. "Don't mind Jade. She's hating that she's got to change schools."

"There's something I wanted to talk to you both about."

"What is it?" Butch asked.

Michael rubbed the back of his head. "I don't want to stay in Fort Wills anymore. I'd like to try out here. You know, become a Prospect. Dad set me up a job with one of the accounting firms he uses. I'll be starting there next week. He wanted to call you before I came out here, but I wanted to be the one to ask. I'd like to come home."

Butch stared at the man before him.

Glancing down at Cheryl, he saw his wife had tears in her eyes.

"What do you think, Cheryl? We want him back? He can't get involved in the wrong crowd now."

Cheryl swatted at his hand. "You know the hardest thing I ever did was to let you go to your father. I hated it. Every single second of it."

"I know why you did it, and I love you, Mom."

"You can join the club. You won't be getting any

special treatment."

"I don't expect any. I'm going to go and grab a beer."

Michael left them alone as Javier, Mistletoe, and Cruz headed toward him.

They were the original four, with Punk following up behind. It had taken Punk a year to earn his patch, but he was a damn good friend and club brother.

"We did it, Butch," Javier said.

"Next, world domination?" Cruz asked.

Glancing around the yard, he saw a mixture of Ned Walker's fighters and club brothers. This was his home.

His brothers.

His family.

The sins of his past were finally gone.

"You okay?" Cheryl asked.

"Yeah, I'm great." He pulled her against him, kissing her lips.

Life was good.

For Butch, that was all he could ask for.

The End

CHRISTMAS COMES BUTCH ONCE A YEAR

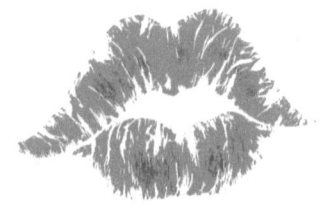

EVERNIGHT PUBLISHING ®

www.evernightpublishing.com